Go West, Darcy!

Book
6

By Laura J. Burns

Based on the television series
created by Tim Maile and Douglas Tuber

Stan Rogow Productions • Grosset & Dunlap

GROSSET & DUNLAP
Published by the Penguin Group
Penguin Group (USA) Inc., 375 Hudson Street, New York, New York 10014, U.S.A.
Penguin Group (Canada), 90 Eglinton Avenue East, Suite 700, Toronto, Ontario,
Canada M4P 2Y3 (a division of Pearson Penguin Canada Inc.)
Penguin Books Ltd, 80 Strand, London WC2R 0RL, England
Penguin Ireland, 25 St Stephen's Green, Dublin 2, Ireland
(a division of Penguin Books Ltd)
Penguin Group (Australia), 250 Camberwell Road, Camberwell, Victoria 3124, Australia
(a division of Pearson Australia Group Pty Ltd)
Penguin Books India Pvt Ltd, 11 Community Centre, Panchsheel Park,
New Delhi - 110 017, India
Penguin Group (NZ), Cnr Airborne and Rosedale Roads, Albany, Auckland 1310,
New Zealand (a division of Pearson New Zealand Ltd)
Penguin Books (South Africa) (Pty) Ltd, 24 Sturdee Avenue, Rosebank, Johannesburg
2196, South Africa

Penguin Books Ltd, Registered Offices:
80 Strand, London WC2R 0RL, England

Published by Grosset & Dunlap, a division of Penguin Young Readers Group, 345
Hudson Street, New York, New York 10014. GROSSET & DUNLAP is a trademark
of Penguin Group (USA) Inc. Printed in the U.S.A.

Library of Congress Cataloging-in-Publication Data
Burns, Laura J.
Go west, Darcy! / by Laura J. Burns ; based on the television series created by Tim
Maile & Douglas Tuber.
p. cm. -- (Darcy's wild life ; 6)
ISBN 0-448-44353-8 (pbk.)
I. Title. II. Series.
PZ7.H22284Go 2006
2006004458

10 9 8 7 6 5 4 3 2 1

Hello!

I'm Sara Paxton, also known as Darcy Fields on <u>Darcy's Wild Life</u>. You are totally going to love the two new books in the <u>Darcy</u> series!

In some ways, Darcy and I are very different, but in others we couldn't be more alike! We both love summertime—cute summer clothes, warm weather, suntans—and we're both a little dramatic.

Luckily, I get my share of drama filming <u>Darcy's Wild Life</u>, but, now that she's been uprooted from Hollywood, Darcy sometimes has to make her own! Bailey turns into Baileywood when Darcy gets involved with the local theater production, and the possibility of a trip back to Tinsel Town has Darcy caught between her two worlds. The simple life? I think not!

I've been playing Darcy for a while now, and boy has my character come a long way! She still misses the excitement—and a little bit of the drama—of her old life in Hollywood, but Darcy absolutely loves her new life in Bailey, livestock included! She's a natural with animals, and, with great friends and a wonderful mom to support her, is it any wonder that this girl can do anything she sets her mind to?

Life is always a walk on the wild side with Darcy, but you can always count on her (and me!) to make the most of it! I'm so excited about all of the adventures in store for Darcy, and I know you will be, too.

I hope you're enjoying the show, and I know you're going to love these books! Thanks for joining me, and happy reading!

Best Wishes!

♡ always,

Sara Paxton

Chapter 1

"High-gloss hoof-moisturizing cream?"

Darcy Fields glanced at her best friend, Lindsay
Adams. "For horses or pigs?" Darcy asked.

"Pigs."

With a sigh, Darcy turned to the stockroom shelf
and began to count the supply of hoof cream. If
anyone had told her a year ago that she'd be spending
her afternoons counting beauty products for pigs, she
would have thought they were delusional. Darcy Fields,
daughter of famous movie star Victoria Fields, simply
didn't *do* things like take inventory. Especially not when
the inventory involved muddy, snorting beasts.

But even though Darcy still liked to complain about
the fact that her mom had moved them from Malibu
to Bailey, a town in the middle of nowhere, the truth

was that she'd grown kind of fond of pigs—and horses, goats, ducks, cows, and any other animals that happened by. Lots of animals happened by when you lived on a ranch in the middle of the wilderness. And when you worked in a veterinarian's office.

"Fifteen tubes of hoof cream," Darcy reported. "And one seriously bored girl."

Lindsay shook her head. "*Two* seriously bored girls," she corrected. She wrote the hoof-cream number on her inventory list, then dropped down onto a stack of dog food bags. "I can't believe it's not even lunchtime yet. This day is going so slowly."

"Is it always this slow in August?" Darcy asked. "Because I might have to take drastic measures if things don't get more interesting around here."

"Like what?" Lindsay asked.

Darcy bit her lip while she thought about it. What would make life in the country more exciting? "Livestock races?" she suggested. "Wait, no. Livestock beauty pageants!" There were more cows in Bailey than people, so she figured there would be plenty of contestants.

Lindsay shook her head. "It's so hot out that even the pigs and cows aren't willing to move much. Although you never know—they might be just as bored as we are."

Darcy slumped onto the pile of food bags next to Lindsay. "I gotta admit, I thought Bailey was a little slow-paced before," she said. "But these past few weeks it's gotten even slower. It's, well . . ."

"Totally, completely dead?" Lindsay's younger brother, Jack, said as he came into the stockroom. "Absolutely the most boring place on earth?"

"I was gonna say 'it's so slow that it's practically stopped,'" Darcy replied.

"You're both right," Lindsay said. "I've never been so bored. The movie theater has been showing the same thing for two months. All of our regular customers are away on vacation. Dad is so bored that he's started napping right along with Snoozie."

Darcy couldn't help a smile at that. For some reason, this one old man was always asleep on a bench in the waiting room of Creature Comforts, the veterinarian's office that Lindsay's father owned. Darcy had never once seen him awake. "Why doesn't your dad close the office?" Darcy asked. "You could all take a trip somewhere fun. We haven't had a single patient show up all week."

Lindsay shrugged. "Dad's the only vet in the area. If something happened and he wasn't here to help, he'd feel terrible."

"I feel terrible that we *are* here," Jack grumbled. "Everyone else obviously realizes that Bailey in August is too dull to stand. Why can't we go on vacation along with the rest of the town?"

"Because the animals come first," Lindsay said. "Besides, it's the perfect time to take inventory. We order all the pet supplies for the year every August."

"But inventory is boring," Darcy pointed out.

"You don't have to tell *me* that." Lindsay scanned the list on her clipboard. "And we haven't even started on the medical supplies yet. Just wait till we start counting cotton gauze pads."

Darcy wanted to go to sleep just thinking about it.

"At least you're making money," Jack pointed out. "I've got a big fat nada."

"You can help us with inventory," Lindsay said. "Dad would probably pay you for that."

Jack raised an eyebrow and stared at her as if she'd grown an extra head. "Inventory?" he snorted.

"It's not as exciting as your usual moneymaking schemes," Darcy admitted. Jack was famous for coming up with crazy ways to make a buck—none of which ever worked. "But it's better than nothing."

"What would *really* be exciting was if your mom threw a big, swanky party," Jack said. "I'd much rather help her plan a Hollywood bash than help you two count Wee-Wee Pads."

"That won't work," Darcy told him. "Mom's Hollywood

friends all go to Europe in August. Not to Bailey."

Jack waved his hand dismissively. "Then she can have a swanky party for the people here," he said. "Either way, she'll pay me to be her assistant. Or maybe she'll let me plan the whole party. Then I can make my name as a famous event planner, and everyone will hire me to choreograph their soirees."

"Uh, Jack?" Lindsay said. "Who exactly is she going to invite? Half the shops in town are closed. Even the diner is shut for the week. Everyone is off having fun somewhere else."

"Except us," Darcy mumbled. "I can't believe that I have the worst social life in Bailey."

"Thanks a lot," Lindsay joked.

Darcy's cheeks heated up. "I mean, I can't believe that *we* have the worst social life in Bailey," she quickly corrected herself. "Believe me, I'd be way more bummed if you weren't around to share the misery."

Lindsay raised one eyebrow. "Is that supposed to make me feel better?"

"Yes," Darcy replied. "Because hanging out and complaining to each other about how bored we are *is* actually kind of fun. So I'm saying that I enjoy being bored with you."

"Thank you. I enjoy being bored with you, too," Lindsay said with a grin.

"Hey, maybe you and I and Kathi can do a sleep-over tomorrow night," Darcy suggested.

"We did that yesterday," Lindsay said.

"I know, but it's still more fun than sitting around watching reruns on TV," Darcy replied. "I can show you how to do that upside-down French-braid thing with your hair."

"I guess." Lindsay didn't sound too psyched about the idea. "But I think we're gonna end up watching reruns on TV anyhow."

"Yeah, but we'll be doing it in a group, which is better," Darcy said.

"How about you do a fancy sleepover party and pay me to plan it?" Jack suggested.

"No!" Darcy and Lindsay hollered.

"Fine. I'll just go play a video game. Again." Jack put on his best hurt look and shuffled out the door.

"Don't worry, we'll find some way to make our sleepover fun," Darcy assured Lindsay. "Maybe we can do a movie marathon. You know, like rent all movies starring Keanu and watch them all in chronological order."

"Keanu?" Lindsay said doubtfully.

"Or all the Disney princess movies?" Darcy suggested. "Or, um, all movies about dogs acting heroic?"

"Or all movies about big giant apes," Lindsay put in.

"No, I know. All movies with the word 'love' in the title," Darcy said. "That should take up about five nights' worth of sleepovers. We'll never be bored again!"

"The way it's been around here lately, we're gonna have to do all movies with the word 'the' in the title," Lindsay joked. "That will take us all the way through to September when everybody comes home and things pick up around here."

Darcy grabbed a piece of hay from one of the feed stacks and began to chew on the end. "We can make snacks to match whichever movie theme we pick," she said, thinking aloud. "Like Hawaiian for Keanu movies, since Keanu is a Hawaiian name. Or hot dogs for the dog movie theme. And maybe those little Valentine hearts for the 'love' movie marathon . . ." She was beginning to get excited about the idea. "And we can watch on my mom's huge flat-screen TV instead of the little TV in the living room," she went on. "We can decorate according to the theme. Ooh! And we can wear outfits that go with the movies!"

Lindsay laughed. "Now you sound like Jack, planning a big fancy sleepover."

Darcy covered her mouth and giggled. "I do sound like Jack. Yikes!"

"Don't worry, I won't tell anyone," Lindsay promised. "But we should get back to work." She checked her inventory list. "Cat toothpaste?"

Darcy yawned as she got up and went over to the cat supplies shelf. "Let's see if I can stay awake to count it all."

Suddenly the most beautiful sound in the world floated through the air—the sound of the bell on the front door of the office. Darcy spun around to look at Lindsay. Her friend's eyes were wide with excitement. "Is that . . . a customer?" Lindsay whispered.

Darcy's mind raced. Maybe it was a customer with several different pets. And maybe all of them needed help. That would keep things busy around Creature Comforts for a few hours! Or it could be just one animal with a really complicated problem. Then Lindsay's dad would need the rest of the day to figure out a treatment, and he'd need Lindsay and Darcy to help. Maybe it could even take *two* days to figure out a treatment . . .

"This could be our ticket out of dullsville," Darcy said. She flew toward the stockroom door, Lindsay on her heels. Out in the waiting room, they ran right into Kevin, Lindsay's father. He was running for the front counter, too. Obviously he was just as happy about the idea of a customer as they were.

"What seems to be the problem?" Kevin cheerfully greeted the two overall-clad guys, Brett and Brandon Brennan, who stood there.

"Do you have a sick animal?" Darcy added eagerly. "Or more than one?" She knew the Brennan brothers rescued and cared for a lot of exotic animals. They had been among the first people Darcy met when she started working at Creature Comforts.

"We sure do," Brandon replied. "Spike here has been vomiting since this morning." He held up a depressed-looking porcupine.

"That's terrible," Lindsay said. "I'll get the exam room ready." She rushed into the examination room while Darcy carefully took the porcupine from Brandon.

"It's okay, little fella," she said. "I'm your friend. Don't stick me!"

"Don't worry about that," Brett told her. "Poor Spike is feeling too awful to put up much of a fight."

"Although you might want to hold his tail down, just in case," Brandon put in. "If he decides to fight you, he'll puff up his quills and hit you with his tail."

"Good to know," Darcy replied, gently holding the porcupine's tail against its side. She carried Spike into the exam room, while Kevin and the Brennans followed.

"When did you first notice Spike getting sick?" Kevin asked.

"About eight this morning," Brett said. "He vomited all over the place, and then he didn't want to touch his breakfast."

"And what did the vomit look like?" Kevin asked.

Darcy wrinkled her nose. She'd never heard anyone sound so psyched about throw-up before.

"It was mostly wood chips," Brett said. "With a little plant life thrown in."

Lindsay finished cleaning the examination table with a disinfectant wipe, and Darcy set the little porcupine on it. Kevin pulled out his stethoscope and started a thorough exam.

The Brennan brothers exchanged a glance.

"Uh . . . we were kinda thinking Spike ate something he shouldn't have," Brandon said. "We found a deck chair all chewed up out on the porch."

"A deck chair?" Darcy cried. "You think he ate a *deck chair*?"

"Porcupines love to eat wood," Lindsay told her.

"So we thought maybe you could just give him something to settle his stomach," Brett said. "He probably doesn't need a whole big exam."

Darcy's heart sank. She'd been thinking Spike and his mystery illness were good for at least a half an hour of something to do. Kevin sighed. "You're sure it was Spike who ate the chair?"

"Pretty sure," Brandon replied.

"Okay. Let me see what I've got for porcupine indigestion," Kevin grumbled, heading off to the supply room.

"Do you want us to give Spike a bath or anything while he's here?" Darcy asked hopefully.

"We could trim his claws," Lindsay offered.

The Brennan brothers laughed. "No, thanks. Rodents aren't big on pedicures," Brett said.

Once Kevin had returned with the medicine, the Brennans took their porcupine and left. Darcy looked out the window until their pickup had disappeared in the distance. "Do you think anybody else will come by today?" she asked.

"I don't think anybody else will come by all week," Lindsay sighed. "We'd better just get back to the inventory."

"Yeah." Darcy followed her slowly into the stock-room, trying to shake off the boredom. She had a feeling it wasn't going to be easy.

"And apparently he ate an entire deck chair," Darcy told her mother that night at dinner. "This little bitty porcupine. He's barely the size of a cat!"

"Porcupines like wood," said Eli, the teen guy who worked on their ranch. "They'll eat your house if you let them."

"Really?" Victoria Fields exclaimed in her famous British accent. "How bizarre!" She smiled and popped a piece of broccoli into her mouth. Victoria was always happy here in Bailey, no matter how boring things got. She'd been looking for a change of pace from her Hollywood lifestyle, and the simple life in Bailey was exactly what she wanted. "Do they eat trees, too?"

"Oh, yeah," Eli said. "They can be a regular menace."

"Well, Spike's not a menace," Darcy asserted. "He's pretty cute, in fact. I just wish he'd stayed around longer at Creature Comforts. He was the only remotely fun thing to happen all day."

"Yeah, Bailey is pretty quiet in the dead of summer," Eli said. "That's why I'm planning to paint the barn next week."

"The *whole* barn?" Victoria asked. "Even the roof?"

"Yep. There's really nothing else to do." Eli shrugged.

"Well." Victoria hesitated for a moment. "Perhaps we'd better surround the barn with hay bales, then. You know, just in case you should happen to fall while you're painting." Darcy could tell that her mother was trying to keep a straight face. The idea of accident-prone Eli climbing all over the barn with red paint in his hands *was* pretty amusing. He could barely tie his shoes without falling over.

"I wish I could find a big project like that to keep me busy," Darcy said with a sigh. "Lindsay and I will probably finish the inventory tomorrow, and then I've got absolutely nothing to do for the next . . . well, for the rest of the summer."

"No plans at all?" her mother asked.

"Nope. I'm completely planless," Darcy replied. "Well, except for a marathon of dog movies. Or maybe Keanu movies."

"The video store is closed," Eli said. "The owners are taking an RV trip to Yellowstone."

Darcy groaned. "How can you close the only video store in town? That should be illegal or something." She slumped back in her chair. "So much for the movie marathon and theme party."

"Well then, it seems I've made the right decision," Victoria said. "I have just the thing to jolt you out of your slump."

Darcy sat up a little straighter. "What is it?"

"Oh, the best thing in the world, darling," her mother said. "I bought you a plane ticket to Los Angeles!"

Chapter 2

Wild Wisdom . . . *A cow's spots are like finger-prints—no two cows have exactly the same pattern of spots.*

To: TruBlue
From: Darcy1
Subject: Yay!

Tru, you're never going to believe what my mom just told me! I'm coming home! I mean, not for good or anything. But I'll be back in Los Angeles this very weekend. I can hardly believe it! No more superslow Bailey summer, at least for a few glorious days. So start planning. I want to do *everything*. Oh, and I want to see *everybody*. And go shopping—you know, *everywhere*. We're gonna have the best weekend of all time!

When Darcy got to Creature Comforts the next morning, both Kevin and Jack were dozing on the bench next to the sleeping guy.

Lindsay didn't look much more alert. "Morning," she grumbled.

"Hi, Darcy!" Kathi Giraldi piped up from behind the counter. "I thought I'd come keep you guys company today."

"Cool," Darcy told her friend. "Because Lindsay and I have run out of things to say to each other."

"I think I've run out of things to say, period," Lindsay joked. "This is the slowest summer ever."

"It's true," Kathi agreed. "I thought it was bad the summer that Mrs. Pepperidge's bake sale was the most exciting thing going, but this is even worse."

"Seriously," Lindsay said. "Even Mrs. Pepperidge went away this year."

"Bummer," Darcy commented. "I could use a chocolate cupcake right about now. Or maybe some delicious éclairs. Or a—"

"We're trying to sleep here," Jack called from the bench.

Lindsay rolled her eyes. "Let's go finish inventory," she said. "Jack can watch the front counter."

"Sleeping," Jack said.

"I think we can nap and man the counter all at once," Kevin put in, opening one eye. "We'll just have to multitask."

Darcy followed Lindsay and Kathi into the stockroom. "You guys are never going to believe this," she told them. "I have the best news!"

"Really? What?" Kathi cried.

"Yeah, don't keep us in suspense," Lindsay said. "*Any* news has to be interesting."

"It is." Darcy bounced up and down in excitement. "My mom bought me a plane ticket to Los Angeles. I'm going home for the weekend!" She looked back and forth between her friends. "Isn't that the coolest?"

Kathi and Lindsay both just gazed back at her.

"I haven't been back to L.A. since Mom moved us here," Darcy went on. "I'll get to see my best friends and my old house and my favorite coffee shop and . . . why aren't you guys smiling?"

Kathi immediately put a smile on her face. "That's really cool, Darcy." She nudged Lindsay with her elbow. "Isn't that cool?"

"Yeah! It's supercool," Lindsay replied quickly.

Darcy narrowed her eyes at her friend. Lindsay was the most down-to-earth, unflappable person she'd ever met. Something wasn't right. *"Supercool?"* she repeated. "Linds, you don't say things like 'supercool.' In fact, you don't say 'super' at all."

"Well, I'm, uh, really excited for you," Lindsay said.

"You are not," Darcy objected. She glanced over at

Kathi, who was staring down at her sneakers. "Neither of you are happy! What's going on?"

Her friends exchanged a guilty look. "We *are* happy for you," Lindsay said slowly. "It's just that . . . well . . ."

"If you go away for the weekend, we'll *really* have nothing to do!" Kathi burst out. "I mean, you'll be off hanging out with all your movie-star friends and having the best time ever. And Lindsay and I will just be sitting here playing Monopoly by ourselves."

"Monopoly?" Darcy asked doubtfully.

"Okay, maybe we'll play Trivial Pursuit. But still, it will be lame," Kathi said.

"Superlame," Lindsay agreed.

"Being bored together is just more fun than being bored alone," Kathi added. "And three bored people are more fun than two bored people."

"Huh." Darcy frowned. "I didn't think of that."

"Yes, you did. You said the same exact thing yesterday," Lindsay told her.

"Oh. Yeah. But I didn't think about how you two would feel if I went." Darcy looked at their sad faces and felt her happiness drain away. "I'm sorry, you guys. I was just so psyched to see L.A. again."

"Don't be sorry, Darcy," Lindsay told her. "You should be psyched. You'll have a great time."

"Yeah," Kathi agreed. "And besides, it's better if one of us has fun than none of us."

Darcy bit her lip. Her friends were being totally sweet. But what if she were the one staying behind while Lindsay went away for the weekend? Or Kathi? She'd be completely depressed. And now that she knew how they felt, how was she supposed to fly off to California and leave them behind?

"And they both tried really hard to act all excited and stuff. But I could tell they were seriously dreading the weekend." Darcy stuffed a forkful of Eli's macaroni salad into her mouth and looked across the table at her mom.

"Nonsense," Victoria said. "I'm sure they understand perfectly and they're very happy for you."

"Well, yeah," Darcy replied. "They're happy for *me*, but they're unhappy for themselves. Even one person makes a big difference in the Bailey social scene these days." She took a deep breath. "Maybe I shouldn't go."

"Not go to Los Angeles?" Victoria placed her hand against Darcy's forehead. "Do you have a fever or something?" she joked.

"I know, I know," Darcy grumbled with a smile. "I'm usually all about wanting to get back to California."

"Not only that," Victoria said. "I thought you'd be missing your friends back on the coast. Don't you want to see Tru? And Riley?"

"Definitely!" Darcy cried. "I can't believe it's been so long since I hung out with them. But what about Lindsay and Kathi? How can I just abandon them?"

"I think they can survive for a few days without you," Victoria said.

"Who?" Eli asked, coming into the dining room with a tray full of homemade pizza cut into animal shapes.

"Whoa, Eli, what's all this?" Darcy cried.

"Zoo pizza," he explained. "I was bored, so I cut the bread into shapes like animal crackers. You like it?" He held the tray up vertically so they could see all the different creatures—and the pizza started sliding off the edge.

Darcy lunged across the table and caught a cheesy giraffe just as it was about to plunge to its doom. "Um, maybe you should put the tray on the table and then we'll look at them," she suggested.

Eli nodded. "Good idea." He placed the tray down and then carefully rearranged all the animal shapes.

"That is truly impressive," Victoria told him.

"It is," Darcy agreed. "But we already scarfed down all the macaroni salad. I didn't know we were having a two-course lunch."

"Are you kidding? I also have homemade potato chips coming. And brownies for dessert," Eli said.

They stared at him in surprise.

"I've been cooking a lot. I'm a little bored," Eli admitted with a shrug.

"Exactly," Darcy said. "And wouldn't you be even more bored if one of us went away for the weekend?"

"I guess," Eli replied. "One less person to talk to."

"See?" Darcy told her mom. "I just can't do it. I can't leave my friends alone."

Victoria looked at her, a serious expression on her beautiful face. "Are you saying you'd rather stay here in Bailey, even when it's dull, than go back to California?"

Darcy thought about it. She loved California. She *missed* California. She missed the perfect weather and the sound of the surf and the crazy energy of Hollywood. And most of all, she missed her friends. But what about her friends here in Bailey? They needed her. They could very possibly die of boredom without her. "Yeah," she said slowly. "I guess I would rather stay here. I mean, since Lindsay and Kathi are stuck here."

"Well. I'm speechless," Victoria said.

"I know." Darcy grinned. "I'm all about the personal growth today! Bet you never thought you'd see me turn down a trip to L.A."

Victoria threw up her hands and laughed. "No, I really never did. And I'll tell you what. Since you've *grown* so much, I'm going to reward you."

"Cool," Darcy said. "You'll get us three different kinds of ice cream for our sleepover tomorrow night?"

"Even better," Victoria said. "I'm going to send Lindsay and Kathi to California with you."

"She said *what*?" Lindsay exclaimed the next morning at Creature Comforts.

"You and Kathi can come with me," Darcy practically sang. "We're gonna have the best time!"

"Wait a minute," Jack said, crossing his arms over his chest. "I'm sure there's some kind of mistake. Your mother meant that Lindsay and *Jack* can go with you. Not Kathi. *Jack*."

Darcy laughed. "Nope. I heard her pretty clearly. And then I made her repeat it, like, ten times."

"Did you tell Kathi?" Lindsay asked.

"Why do you think I was late this morning?" Darcy said. "She didn't stop talking for about half an hour straight after I gave her the good news." She grinned at the memory. One thing Kathi was good at was talking!

"And your mom is really going to pay for us to go? Isn't that expensive?" Lindsay asked with a frown.

"Hello, she's a famous movie star," Jack put in. "She's rich."

"That doesn't mean she should be paying for other people to do whatever they want," Lindsay told him.

"It was her idea. She wants to do it," Darcy insisted. "Believe me. It's totally okay."

"Wow," Lindsay said slowly. "Los Angeles. I've never been there."

"You'll love it," Darcy said. "And you'll get to meet my best friends. Well, my best California friends. Tru and Riley. They're so much fun—I already e-mailed Tru this morning so she can start making plans for us."

Lindsay was grinning widely. "I can't wait! I have to go online and research L.A. before we leave."

"Who needs research? You've got a native to show you everything worth seeing," Darcy said.

"Yeah, but I still need to do my homework on the place. You know me."

"I wouldn't be that high-maintenance, Darcy," Jack said. "I'd let you show me around."

"Jack, you're not coming with us," Lindsay told him.

"I have a hard time believing that Victoria wouldn't send me with you," he argued. "She loves me!"

"That's why she needs you to stay here," Darcy said. "How could she get through the weekend without you? Especially with me gone, too."

Jack opened his mouth, but he couldn't think of anything else to say. Finally he just stomped out of the waiting room with a groan.

"You guys!" Kathi gushed, rushing through the front door. "Guess what? My dad said I could take the camcorder with me! I'll be able to film our entire trip to Hollywood!"

"Cool," Darcy said. "But—"

"Oh, and my mom said she'll take me shopping tomorrow for beach clothes. I've never been to a beach! I mean, I've been to the beach by the lake, but that's not a real beach. Is it?"

"I think—" Lindsay began.

"Well, it's not an *ocean* beach, anyway," Kathi went on. "I've never seen the ocean. Will there be surfers?"

"Usually at—" Darcy started.

"Cool! I'll film them with the camcorder. And then maybe I can, like, interview some of them just so I'll have footage of actual California surfers . . ."

Lindsay raised her eyebrows and shot Darcy a smile. It was clear that neither one of them would be getting a word in anytime soon. Darcy decided to take drastic action. "Orlando Bloom likes to surf," she said.

Kathi's eyes widened and her mouth dropped open. Darcy figured they had about five seconds before she started to talk again.

"So, listen," Darcy said quickly. "We need to plan.

Mom booked us on a plane that leaves Friday morning. Which means we'll be in L.A. by noon. Which means we have Friday afternoon through Sunday night to do anything we want."

"Which means we have to get to work right now," Lindsay said. "Sorry to be the boring one, but we've still got half the inventory to do."

"No problem. I'll help you," Kathi said.

"When you helped us yesterday, all we did was talk all day, and we got nothing done," Darcy pointed out.

"I promise I will not talk unless it's about veterinary supplies," Kathi said.

"You don't have to help us. It's not *your* job," Lindsay told her.

Kathi grabbed Lindsay's clipboard. "I'm definitely helping. Because the sooner you two finish work, the sooner we can all go shopping for our California trip!"

TruBlue: Hey, chiquita! So psyched you're coming today! Are you at the airport?

Darcyı: Nope. I'm at the breakfast table. Waffles, yum!

TruBlue: Riley and I are meeting up after her yoga class to go to your hotel. BTW, we're totally set for our spa day. I reserved five spots at Georgette.

Darcy: OMG, I'm so psyched! I haven't had a facial since I moved here. Unless you count falling in the mud of a pigsty.

TruBlue: Um . . . gross.

Darcy: The spa day is a surprise for Lindsay and Kathi, though. Don't tell.

TruBlue: Lips sealed. Can't wait to meet them!

Darcy: We're gonna have so much fun.

TruBlue: I can't believe we're going to see you TODAY!!

TruBlue: Darcy?

TruBlue: Hello??

Darcy: Sorry, I just heard a horn outside. Gotta go. See you soon!! :)

Darcy shoved her Blackberry into its belt holster and jumped up from the table. "Was that a horn?" she asked eagerly, running to the window. "Did you hear a horn?"

"No, sweetie. I heard a moo," Victoria replied, taking a sip of coffee. "Kevin isn't supposed to be here for another ten minutes."

"I know," Darcy sighed. "But Lindsay is always early everywhere, so I thought maybe she made her dad, you know, drive faster."

Victoria smiled. "I know you're excited about your trip, but you have to be a little bit patient. No nagging Kevin to speed up just to get you to the airport more quickly. It's very sweet of him to drive you girls."

"And it's a good thing he's willing to," Darcy agreed. "I don't think my luggage would fit in any of our cars." She glanced over at the four huge suitcases sitting by the door. "Do you think I need to bring another pair of shoes to go with my blue capris?"

"You already have three pairs to choose from," Victoria said. "I imagine that will be enough."

Darcy frowned, running over all the outfits in her mind. She and Tru had made some plans for things to do during her visit, but she wanted to be prepared for anything else that came up, too. "Maybe I should bring some hiking boots," she said.

Victoria raised her eyebrows. "You have two and a half days in L.A. Do you really think you'll be going hiking?"

"You never know," Darcy said. "Riley and I went hiking once."

"And if I recall correctly, you phoned me from the

trail and asked me to send a helicopter to pick you up because you were tired," Victoria said.

"Yeah, but you didn't, so we had to walk all the way back," Darcy replied. "That counts as a hike."

A car horn blared outside, and she jumped. "They're here! That was definitely not a moo."

"Not unless one of the cows has developed a severe head cold," Victoria agreed.

Darcy yanked open the door just as Kevin's pickup truck pulled into the driveway. She'd never seen a more beautiful sight. She was about to head off on an adventure—no more Bailey, no more boredom! She'd get to see her old friends *and* hang with her new friends. And it was all about to start . . . right now!

Jack climbed out of the truck and trudged over to the door. "Morning," he grumbled.

"Why, Jack, whatever is the matter?" Victoria asked.

He gave her his most pathetic shrug. "I'm just going to miss Lindsay so much," he said. "We're very close, you know. I don't think we've ever been apart for this long."

"That's so sad!" Victoria cried. "Tell you what. You and I will rent a movie tomorrow night. We'll make popcorn and everything. That way you won't feel so lonely."

"The video store is closed," Jack said. "Maybe you could just send me to California with Lindsay."

Victoria tried to hide her smile. "If I did that, your father would be the lonely one. Isn't that right, Kevin?"

Kevin, Lindsay, and Kathi had all piled out of the truck and come over to the door.

"Absolutely. I can't spend an entire weekend missing *both* my kids," Kevin said.

Jack looked back and forth between them, trying to think of another angle to try. "But think of what an opportunity it could be, Dad," he said. "You're always saying you want to finish reading *Moby Dick*, but you can't find the time. With Lindsay and me both out of the way, you'll have plenty of hours for reading."

"Give it up, Jack," Lindsay said, messing up his longish brown hair. "You're not coming."

Jack turned to Darcy. She shook her head. "No way."

With a growl of frustration, he stomped inside to hang with Eli in the kitchen.

"Ready to go, Darcy?" Kevin asked.

"Are you kidding?" she cried. "I've been ready for *hours*. I woke up at four thirty in the morning!"

"Me too," Kathi said. "I repacked my suitcase about twenty times. I hope I didn't forget anything."

"I know what you mean," Darcy said. "Maybe I

34

should do one last check around my room."

Victoria stepped into the doorway, blocking Darcy's path back to the stairs. "You've brought more than enough, sweetie."

"Let's get going, then," Kevin said. He eyed the suitcases near the door. "Which one is yours, Darcy?"

"All of them."

"*All* of them?" Lindsay cried. "You're bringing four suitcases for two days?"

"Two and a half days," Darcy said. "Why? How many are you bringing?"

"I have my mother's really huge suitcase," Kathi declared. "Oh, plus the camcorder. And three other cameras. So with all the camera bags, I have five bags. I win!"

"Camera bags are small. Darcy's suitcases are all big," Lindsay pointed out.

"Lindsay doesn't even have a real suitcase," Kathi told Darcy. "Just a carry-on."

"It's only two days!" Lindsay said. "How much stuff could I possibly need?"

While they were talking, Kevin had dragged one suitcase out to the pickup and hurled it into the back. He came limping back to the front door, rubbing his back. "I think I'm gonna need some help with the rest," he said ruefully. "Is Eli here?"

Between him and Eli, with a little help from the girls, they managed to get all four suitcases into the truck.

Darcy gave her mother a big hug. "Thank you, thank you, thank you!" she said. "This is going to be my favorite vacation ever."

"You girls have a wonderful time," Victoria told them as they all climbed into the cab of the pickup.

"We will," Darcy replied. "California, here we come!"

Chapter 3

Wild Wisdom . . . *There are over four hundred
breeds of domestic dogs.*

"Darcy!" Kathi whispered, pulling Darcy aside in the
busy hallway of the Los Angeles International Airport.
"That guy is looking for you. Are we in trouble?"

Darcy scanned the crowd of people waiting near the
baggage carousels. A tall African-American man in a blue
jacket held up a sign that said "Darcy Fields."

"That's Andre!" Darcy cried. She grabbed her
friends' hands and tugged them over to him.

"D-girl!" he said, a wide grin spreading across his
face. "What's up, lady?"

Darcy threw her arms around him. "Did my mom call
you?"

"You know it," Andre said. "She told me you were
coming for the weekend, so I freed up my limo just for
you."

"You're driving us all weekend?" Darcy asked.

Andre nodded. "I'm totally at your service. Don't tell me . . . Lindsay," he added, turning to Lindsay.

Her eyes widened. "How did you know?"

"Victoria said Darcy was traveling with a no-nonsense type and a stargazer. I'm thinking you're the no-nonsense type, and that makes you Lindsay."

Lindsay's pale cheeks reddened, and Darcy, Andre, and Kathi laughed. "I guess that makes me the star-gazer," Kathi said. "Do you think I'll actually get to see anyone famous?"

"You kidding?" Andre said. "It's Hollywood. You'll see *tons* of famous people. But you know Victoria Fields. Meeting movie stars is nothing new to you."

"We only know one movie star," Lindsay said. "And Darcy's mom is so laid-back that she doesn't seem like a star."

"I hear you," Andre agreed. "Victoria and Darcy were my favorite clients. I've been missing them."

"And we miss you," Darcy said. "Why don't you move to Bailey and drive us around there?"

Andre grinned. "You know I'm a city boy, Darce. Now let's go get your bags."

"Darcy brought four huge suitcases," Lindsay warned him.

"Of course she did," Andre replied. "That's why I grabbed a cart." He stepped aside to show them one of the metal pushcarts that the airport supplied. "Shall we?"

Darcy followed him with a contented sigh. It was so good to see Andre again—he'd always been her favorite driver. It was even good to see LAX again—it was her favorite airport! She glanced outside at the traffic and the palm trees and got a warm, happy feeling all up and down her body. It was great to be home!

"Omigosh, it's *huge!*" Kathi cried as soon as Andre closed the limo door. "Is this like a superduper stretch limo or something?"

"It's just a normal limo," Darcy replied, pulling out her cell phone.

"Why do we need a limo?" Lindsay asked quietly. "Your mom shouldn't have to pay somebody to drive us around all weekend."

Darcy raised her eyebrows. "Didn't your research tell you how spread out Los Angeles is? You need a car to get around."

"We could take a bus or something," Lindsay said. "I feel bad having Andre drive us."

"That's his job, silly," Darcy told her. "Don't worry so much." She hit the speed-dial number for Tru's cell phone and waited for it to connect.

"I need my camcorder," Kathi said frantically as they pulled out of the airport parking garage.

"Why?" Lindsay asked.

"I want to film the drive to the hotel," Kathi replied, unpacking the camera.

"Darcy!" Tru's voice came through the phone.

"Hi!" Darcy cried. "We're here! We landed twenty minutes ago." She glanced over just as Kathi finished lowering the automatic window and pointed the camcorder outside. "There's nothing interesting to see until we get into Hollywood," Darcy told her.

"Huh?" Tru asked.

"Sorry, Tru. Hang on a sec," Darcy said. She tapped Kathi on the arm. "You're wasting film. It's all just freeway."

"Yeah, but it's California freeway," Kathi said. "We don't have roads this big at home."

Lindsay shook her head at Darcy as if to say she shouldn't bother. Kathi was obviously going to film the entire weekend no matter what they said.

"Darcy?" Tru asked.

"Oh! Sorry," Darcy said into the phone. "I forgot about you."

"Thanks a lot," Tru replied. "Listen, I'm gonna conference Riley in."

"Cool." Darcy glanced over at Kathi, who was practically hanging out the window filming.

"Look at that car!" Kathi cried. "My dad would love it. It's probably from the fifties." A hot pink vintage car with fins on the back slowly passed them, and Darcy smiled. She'd forgotten how many people out here had great old cars like that.

"Darce!" Riley's voice came through the phone. "Is that you?"

"Hey, girl!" Darcy cried. "Are we all on now?"

"Yup," Tru said.

"Just like the old days," Riley added.

"How was yoga?" Darcy asked.

"So hard!" Riley said. "Do you remember Kefre?"

"Totally. She's the most brutal teacher ever," Darcy said. "Once she made me stay in downward dog for ten minutes straight."

Lindsay was staring at her as if she were crazy.

"What?" Darcy said.

"What?" Riley and Tru asked together.

"Nothing," Lindsay said with a sigh.

"Um . . . nothing," Darcy said into the phone. "So you had Kefre?"

"Yeah. She kicked my butt," Riley said. "I'm so into yoga these days, Darce, you won't believe it. I've been going every day all summer."

"As long as you're not too tired to play all weekend," Darcy said.

"Why do you think she's so into the spa day?" Tru said. "Girl needs a massage."

"I cannot wait," Riley said.

"Me neither," Darcy tried to keep the big smile off her face. Kathi and Lindsay were going to be so psyched when she told them about her surprise spa plan.

"Omigosh, here we go. We're getting off the freeway," Kathi cried. "Now we'll see some good L.A. sights."

"Yeah, check it out, there's a McDonald's," Lindsay joked. "Ooh, and a Gap!"

Darcy laughed. "Yeah, there are plenty of those."

"Plenty of what?" Tru asked.

"Oh, sorry, I was talking to Lindsay," Darcy replied. "So, where are you guys now?"

"At Virgin Records," Tru said. "Riley's buying a DVD, and then we're gonna walk over to your hotel."

"Ooh, what are you buying?" Darcy asked.

"*Pretty Woman,*" Riley said. "The dog ate my old copy of it."

"Duchess!" Darcy cried. "How is she?"

"Cute as ever," Riley replied.

"We're turning onto Sunset Boulevard," Kathi announced. "Is that *the* Sunset Boulevard?"

"Yup," Darcy replied. "The one and only. We're coming up to the Sunset Strip."

"No way. I have to get a better view of that," Kathi

said. She glanced up at the ceiling. "Hey, does that sunroof open?"

"Of course," Darcy said. "You just—"

"Hey, Darce, did you say you're on the Strip already?" Tru cut in. "We better boogie or we won't make it to the Standard before you do."

Lindsay had discovered the controls and opened the sunroof.

"Perfect!" Kathi climbed up on the seat and stuck her head and shoulders out the roof to film.

"Whoa!" Darcy cried, surprised. "Get down."

"What?" Riley said. "Why?"

"Not you," Darcy replied. She tugged frantically at Kathi's leg, trying to get her attention. "Kathi!"

"What?" Kathi said from outside the car.

"Get down!" Darcy called up to her. She couldn't believe Kathi was actually hanging out the sunroof. Nobody Darcy knew in California would do something like that. Darcy really wanted her Bailey friends to fit in out here, but Kathi was going to embarrass herself on their first day!

"Why? I can see everything from up here," Kathi said. "Look! There's the Viper Room!"

"Um, Darce?" Tru said into the phone. "Did you just drive past the Viper Room?"

"With someone sticking out of your car?" Riley added.

Darcy cringed. There it was—Kathi embarrassing herself. "Yes," she admitted.

"What's wrong?" Lindsay asked her.

"They just saw Kathi sticking out of the car," Darcy replied miserably.

"So what?" Lindsay asked.

"It's . . . it's just . . . kind of . . . not done," Darcy said. But Kathi was doing it. Darcy took a deep breath. So what if Riley and Tru had seen Kathi acting weird? They'd understand.

"Darce, we'll see you in, like, two minutes," Riley said into the phone.

"Okay, you guys! I'll see you in the lobby!" Darcy hit END on her cell and shoved it back into her purse, bouncing up and down in her seat. She couldn't wait to see her old friends.

"Did you just say they're meeting us in the lobby?" Lindsay asked.

"Yup."

"So why did you have to talk to them on the phone for so long?" Lindsay looked baffled.

"Because . . ." Darcy couldn't really think of a reason. It had never even occurred to her that she needed a reason. "Um, because that's just what we do."

"The Standard. Is that our hotel?" Kathi called down to them. "Why is the sign upside down?"

Darcy grinned. "Because that's what makes it cool," she called back.

"An upside down sign?" Lindsay asked. She glanced back and forth between Darcy's face and Kathi's legs. "You guys are just weird."

"Victoria Fields?" the tall blond girl at the hotel desk said. "As in, *Love Has No Name*? As in, *Megumbo*?"

"Yup, that's my mom," Darcy replied. "She reserved a room for us."

"Let me check," the girl said. "Yes, here it is, Ms. Fields."

"Call me Darcy," Darcy said with a smile. "What's the room like?"

"It's a suite on the top floor," the girl told her. "Best room in the place."

"Darcy," Lindsay murmured from behind her. "There's a person in that window." Darcy glanced up at the long, skinny glass box set in the wall behind the desk. A model lay on a lounge chair inside the box, staring out into the lobby with the perfect bored expression on her face.

"Yeah," Darcy said. "There's always somebody in there. It's kind of their signature thing here."

"But it's an actual person," Lindsay said, her

eyebrows drawn together in confusion. "Why is she there?"

"Um . . . for decoration," Darcy explained. "It's sort of like a living decoration."

"We're just supposed to watch some model sitting around in a box?" Lindsay asked. "Why?"

"Because it's cool?" Kathi guessed.

"You got it," Darcy told her. "Can you have a bell-hop bring our bags up to the room?" she asked the desk clerk.

"Of course. Right away," the girl said. "Anything you want, Ms. Fields."

"Darcy!" a voice bellowed.

Darcy turned to see Tru and Riley coming through the front doors. Tru raced across the lobby, her tanned arms outstretched, while Riley followed more slowly. "Tru-Tru!" Darcy squealed, rushing to meet her friend for a hug. They jumped up and down in unison as they embraced. Darcy let go of her and threw her arms around Riley with another squeal.

"Look at your hair!" Darcy cried, pulling away. "It's so long."

"I know," Riley replied, pushing her silky dark hair over her shoulder. "It's been that way for a while, though. Has it really been that long since I've seen you?"

"Yes," Darcy moaned. "It's been forever. I can't believe I missed your hair growing out."

"Yeah, what a tragedy," Lindsay joked.

Riley's eyes widened in surprise. "I'm sorry?" she asked.

"Oh, Lindsay's just kidding," Darcy said quickly. "Right, Linds?"

"Right," Lindsay said. "Sorry. I didn't mean to interrupt your reunion."

"No, I'm being rude," Darcy said. "Lindsay, this is Riley, and this is Tru, my two best friends from home. And you guys, this is Lindsay and . . . Where's Kathi?"

She turned and scanned the room. Where had Kathi gone?

"Is that her?" Tru asked, her voice hushed. She nodded toward one of the rounded black couches scattered around the lobby. Sure enough, there was Kathi. And she was taking a picture of a handsome man with dark hair and a dimple in his left cheek. Darcy's heart sank. She had a bad feeling that Kathi was about to commit another faux pas. She really should have given her Bailey friends a lesson on what was cool and not cool in Los Angeles. How were they supposed to fit in without the proper coolness training?

"What is she doing?" Darcy asked, although she was afraid she knew the answer already.

"Who is that guy?" Lindsay said.

"It's Dylan Strong," Riley murmured. "From *Gold Coast.*"

"Does she know him?" Tru asked.

"Only from watching the soap," Darcy said. She watched, mortified, as Kathi whipped out a little pink notebook and handed it to Dylan Strong.

"Is she asking for his autograph?" Tru asked. "Darcy, stop her!"

Darcy walked toward Kathi as fast as she could without *looking* as if she was in a hurry. It would only call more attention to Kathi if Darcy went running across the lobby, and she didn't want to embarrass her poor friend any more. She heard Lindsay coming up behind her. "Hey, Kath," Darcy called when she got close enough. "We should—"

"Darcy," Kathi chirped. "Look, it's Dylan Strong!"

The soap star flashed Darcy a blindingly white smile.

"Um, hi," Darcy said. "Kathi, let's go."

"Wait, can you take a picture of me with Dylan?" Kathi asked. She turned to Dylan. "Do you mind?"

"Of course not," he said.

Kathi shoved her camera toward Darcy, and Darcy automatically backed away. It was bad enough that

Kathi had asked for an autograph right in the lobby of a popular hotel. But for Darcy to be seen taking a picture of a celebrity? Her reputation would never recover from it!

"Oh, give me the camera," Lindsay said, stepping up from behind her. She grabbed the camera and pointed it at Kathi and Dylan. "Ready?"

Dylan Strong put his arm around Kathi's shoulders, and Kathi's already wide grin grew even wider. Lindsay snapped the photo.

"Thank you so much!" Kathi gushed. "You're totally my favorite soap character."

"No problem," Dylan said.

Darcy grabbed Kathi's arm and pulled her away. "What are you doing?" she asked. "You can't just walk up to somebody like that."

"But I watch *Gold Coast* every day," Kathi said. "He looks even taller in person. Are all actors taller in person? 'Cause your mother is, too."

"Kathi, you're not supposed to bother celebrities," Darcy said.

"Why not?" Kathi asked, her face going pale. "I didn't think I was *bothering* him."

"You weren't," Lindsay put in. "He seemed really nice, and he didn't look annoyed at all. Don't worry about it."

Darcy bit her lip. She hadn't meant to upset Kathi.

And Dylan Strong really hadn't seemed to mind. But it was still embarrassing that Kathi had approached him. "No, I didn't mean that you actually bothered him," Darcy assured her friend. "I meant . . . it's just that Hollywood is full of famous people, and if you go running up to all of them, you'll look kind of uncool."

"Who cares?" Lindsay asked, but Kathi looked even more upset.

"It's like saying that the celebrities are cooler than you just because they're famous," Darcy explained. The truth was, she'd never really thought this much about it before. It was simply understood that you didn't treat famous people any differently. At least it was understood among her Los Angeles friends.

"But he *is* cooler than me," Kathi said, confused. "He's a soap star."

"Yeah, but . . ." Darcy didn't know how to put it. "He's still just a guy."

"To you, maybe," Lindsay said. "You grew up around famous people. That's why you think they're so normal. The rest of us aren't used to seeing celebrities walking around acting like regular people."

"Yeah," Kathi said quietly. "Dylan Strong isn't 'just a guy.'"

"That's true," Darcy replied. "I guess I am more

used to it than you are. But I want you to fit in here. And people from L.A. wouldn't go up and ask for his autograph. Only tourists do that."

Kathi and Lindsay stared at her for a moment. "What?" Darcy asked.

"We *are* tourists," Lindsay pointed out.

Darcy's mouth fell open. She hadn't thought of that.

"Ms. Fields?" a bellhop asked, coming over with their suitcases on a cart. "Are you ready to go up to your room?"

"Yes," Lindsay said. "I can't wait to wash my face. I feel all grimy from the plane." She and Kathi followed the bellhop to the elevators.

Darcy turned to see Riley and Tru still standing near the front doors, watching her and her Bailey friends. They both looked a little embarrassed. She trudged over to them. "Sorry about that," she said. "Kathi's so excited to be in Hollywood."

"But why was she talking to Dylan Strong?" Tru asked.

"She's a big fan of his," Darcy explained. "I think she just figured if he was there, she should go over and tell him how much she loves him."

Riley frowned in confusion. "But he must be so sick of people doing that. He probably just wants to live his life like a normal person."

"I don't know," Darcy said slowly. "My mom never minded when fans came up and talked to her. It just never occurred to me to act all excited about somebody famous."

"Well, why would you?" Tru asked. "They're still only people. They just have cool jobs, that's all."

"I know that, and *you* know that," Darcy said. "But maybe if you don't grow up around famous people, you think there's something different about them. Anyway, Kathi didn't even know she wasn't supposed to talk to Dylan Strong. She's psyched she got a picture with him."

Tru and Riley glanced at each other awkwardly. "Well . . . good," Tru said. "I'm glad she's happy."

"Right," Riley put in. "I guess that's a good way to start her stay in Hollywood."

"Yeah." Darcy couldn't shake the feeling that her old friends were a little weirded out by Kathi's behavior. Because she was weirded out by it, too. It had never even occurred to her that her Bailey friends would act so differently out here in Los Angeles. And yet she kind of understood Kathi's point of view—there wasn't much chance of getting an actor's autograph back in Bailey. She might as well take advantage of being in Hollywood and seeing famous people. Darcy sighed. It was all so complicated. Who was she supposed to defend?

I'll just act as if everything is normal, she decided.
*And maybe Tru and Riley will figure that everything
really is normal. Maybe I'm imagining all the tension.*
She put on her brightest smile. "So . . . do you guys
want to come up to the room?"

Tru glanced over at the elevator, doubt clouding
her eyes. "Maybe you and your friends should get
settled in first."

Riley gestured to her yoga clothes. "Besides, I
should go home and take a shower. I think I'll just
meet you guys at the restaurant tonight. We're still
going to Nobu, right?"

"Definitely," Darcy said. "I have been dying for a
piece of their seared tuna."

"I'm gonna go home and change, too," Tru said. "I
got this supercute dress to wear for tonight—wait till
you see it!"

"Where'd you get it?" Darcy asked.

"Fred Segal. It was—"

"Darce, I think your friends are waiting for you,"
Riley interrupted.

Darcy gasped. "Oops! I better run. See you later, I
guess."

"Yeah. Later," Riley said awkwardly.

Tru gave Darcy a little smile. "Welcome home."

"Thanks." Darcy turned and hurried over to

where the bellhop was holding the elevator door open. Somehow this just didn't feel like a homecoming so far.

"You could clean out the cages in the hospital room," Kevin said on Friday afternoon. "You know, take them outside and really hose them down good."

Jack stared at his father as if he'd lost his mind. "Why would I want to do that?" he asked.

"Well, you've been moping around ever since I got back from the airport. I thought maybe you were bored," Kevin said.

"Of course I'm bored. Everybody's bored. Even *you're* bored," Jack told him. "The only people who aren't bored right now are Lindsay, Darcy, and Kathi." He gave a dramatic sigh. If he couldn't get a free trip to California like his sister, he could at least get a little sympathy.

"You could organize that new shipment of reptile products we just got," Kevin suggested.

Once again, Jack stared at him. "Dad," he said slowly, as if talking to a little baby, "I don't want to do work. Work is even more boring than just sitting around being bored."

"I'll pay you ten bucks," Kevin offered.

Jack considered that. Ten bucks wasn't a bad deal. "Well, I guess—"

Suddenly the door to Creature Comforts flew open, its bell jangling wildly. A woman with thick red hair in an unruly bun came rushing in. "Help!" she cried when she saw Kevin. "I've got a situation here."

"Annie, what's wrong?" Kevin asked.

"Did somebody's dog get loose?" Jack guessed. Annie McCormick ran the only pet boarding facility in the county. If she had an escaped pet, it would at least offer a little excitement for the afternoon.

"Worse. Somebody's dog got sick," she said. Her eyes went to Kevin, desperate. "I think . . . I'm afraid it's distemper."

Kevin paled. "What makes you think that?" he asked, his voice serious. Jack knew that distemper was one of the worst viruses a dog could get.

"He's a rescued dog—his owners found him in the woods a week ago, and they just dropped him off for the weekend. They already had plans to go away, and they weren't expecting to have a dog!"

"So he hasn't been immunized," Kevin said.

"I vaccinated him right away when he arrived, but it's possible that he'd already been infected with the virus," Annie told him. "You know those woods— there are coons and foxes out there. He could've picked it up from any of them."

"Have you isolated him?" Kevin asked.

"Distemper is extremely contagious."

She nodded. "I put him in one of the grooming rooms all by himself, poor pooch. But I've got a real problem here, Doc. My kennel is absolutely full. Everybody and his neighbor are away this week. I've got dogs, cats, rabbits, lizards . . . you name it. If this dog's really got distemper, all the rest of them are in danger of getting it, too."

Kevin nodded grimly. "Let's hope it's just a case of pneumonia or gastroenteritis," he said. "Something I can treat."

"Can you come right away?" Annie asked.

"Absolutely," Kevin said. "Jack, get my bag."

Jack ran into the exam room and grabbed his father's house-call bag. It looked as if the weekend wouldn't be so boring in Bailey after all.

Chapter 4

Wild Wisdom . . . *Foxes are monogamous, usually mating for life, and the father helps the mother raise the young.*

"This restaurant is in Malibu?" Lindsay asked on Friday evening. "Isn't that where you're really from, Darce?"

"Yup," Darcy said from the giant silver beanbag chair in the corner of the hotel suite's living room. She held a compact mirror up to her face while she put on some lip gloss. "It's pretty far from here, actually. A forty-five-minute drive. I think Mom figured we'd have more fun staying here than we would in Malibu."

"How come?"

"Well, Malibu is more of a beach town. Or just big mansions and stuff," Darcy explained. "But here we're in the middle of Hollywood, on the Sunset Strip. There are all kinds of places to hang out, and you can do a lot of people-watching."

"Oh, you mean *tourist* stuff?" Lindsay teased.

"Yeah." Darcy frowned. Obviously her mom had realized that Kathi and Lindsay were actual tourists before she had.

"You guys, everything I put on looks terrible in this mirror," Kathi complained, coming out of the bathroom dressed in a cute skirt and a pink T-shirt. "I look all sunburned or something."

"That's only because the whole bathroom is done in orange," Darcy told her. "The color is reflecting off your clothes. You don't really look sunburned."

"What's up with that bathroom?" Lindsay asked. "Why is it that color?"

"It's sort of a modern art-deco look," Darcy told her. "Isn't it cool?"

"Totally," Kathi said.

"Except for the weird reflection thing that makes you look orange," Lindsay said.

"Well, yeah," Kathi said. "But this whole room is so modern and funky. There's nothing like this in Bailey. I took pictures of all of it. I need to get some more film."

"Already?" Darcy laughed. "You're gonna have five albums full of photos from just this one weekend."

Kathi wasn't listening, though. She was busy checking out her outfit in the mirror over the desk. "I still don't like this. My shirt is boring."

"You've already changed it three times," Lindsay said. "It looks fine."

"But I don't want to look fine. I want to look *good*," Kathi said. "Aren't we going to a restaurant where lots of movie stars hang out, Darcy?"

"Yup," Darcy said. "Nobu is one of the major hot spots."

"See? I need to look amazing. Help me, you guys." Kathi flopped down on the couch and groaned.

"Don't look at me," Lindsay said. "I'm wearing jeans like a normal person."

"I know—you can borrow one of my shirts," Darcy offered. "I brought plenty of extra ones."

"Seriously?" Kathi perked up a little. "Do you have anything that'll make me look all Hollywood?"

"I could probably whip up a Hollywood-premiere-worthy outfit," Darcy replied. "See, Linds, that's why I needed four suitcases!" She went into the bedroom and began pulling out shirts. "So, your skirt has that great floral pattern around the hem. The trick is to pick up one color from that pattern for your top and then accessorize using one of the other colors."

"Okay," Kathi said, following her into the bedroom. "There are pink flowers and green leaves."

"I need more specifics," Darcy sang, searching for pink tops. "Is it baby pink, dark pink, hot pink? Rose-petal pink?"

"Um . . . dark pink, I guess," Kathi said, staring at her skirt. "Kind of purplish-pink."

"Voilà!" Darcy yanked a dark pink silk Armani shell from the suitcase and tossed it to Kathi. "Here's the perfect top. Put it on."

"Good. Can we go now?" Lindsay asked from the living room.

"No!" Darcy protested. "We still have to accessorize. And then maybe put Kathi's hair in an updo."

"Really? You know how to do that?" Kathi asked, pulling on the Armani shirt.

"Sure," Darcy said. She grabbed another suitcase and dug out her traveling jewelry case. "Now we need jewelry that picks up the green tones of the leaves. I'm pretty sure I brought my jade earrings . . ."

"You guys," Lindsay called. "You've been getting ready for dinner for an hour now. It can't possibly take this long to put on clothes."

Darcy stuck her head back out into the living room. Lindsay sat slumped on the couch staring at the flat-screen TV. She looked bored. "Want me to create a Hollywood outfit for you, too?" she asked. Lindsay was wearing her usual jeans-and-T-shirt combo with her hair in a ponytail. She looked cute, the way she always did, but it would be fun to dress her up like a starlet.

"No," Lindsay said emphatically. "I don't need to look all special just to go eat dinner."

"But it's a trendy restaurant," Kathi weighed in. "Everybody else is gonna look like a supermodel."

"Well, I don't need to compete with the models," Lindsay replied. "And it would be nice to talk about something other than what we look like."

"Oh, come on, getting ready is half the fun of going out," Darcy said.

"Not for me," Lindsay said with a resigned grin. "I'm so bored, I might as well be back in Bailey."

"I'm telling you, Eli, things are downright exciting around here," Jack said into the phone at McCormick's McBoardinghouse. "Dad's in there with the patient right now. And Annie says some of the other dogs have suspicious symptoms, too. She's afraid that the distemper may have spread."

"So you won't be back at Creature Comforts anytime soon?" Eli said from the other end.

"Probably not at all today," Jack replied. "Dad was wondering if you could swing by and put a note on the door. You know, just in case anybody comes looking for him."

"I don't think there's anybody left in town to look for him," Eli said. "But I'll go over there now."

"Thanks." Jack hung up and went back into the grooming room to check on his father and the sick dog. "How's it looking?" he asked.

"Well, Bingo has a fever, his eyes are inflamed, and his nose is running," Kevin said. "Plus, he's making chewing movements—it's a type of seizure."

"Huh?" Jack asked.

"Dogs with distemper usually develop a secondary infection that affects them neurologically," Kevin said. "The seizures are a symptom of that."

Jack shook his head. "Dad, it's *Jack*. You're not talking to Lindsay. You have to speak English."

"Oh. Sorry." Kevin ran his hand through his hair. "It looks as if Bingo probably does have distemper. It's very difficult to diagnose, but my feeling is that he's got it."

"Yikes," Jack said. "Poor dog." He'd been hoping Bingo had something less serious. "What's going to happen to him?"

"I hate to say it, but a lot of dogs with distemper end up dying," Kevin said with a sigh.

Annie came in, frowning. "I've got three other dogs down," she announced. "All three have runny noses and eyes; one of them is vomiting, and the other two have diarrhea."

"Okay, they'll have to be quarantined, too," Kevin said. "Get them away from the rest of the animals as soon as possible."

"I'm not sure how to do that, Doc," Annie replied. "I don't have any free cages. This is the only room where I can really keep them separate, and it's not big enough for four dogs. We can't take care of them in here."

"So we have to bring them over to Creature Comforts," Jack said. "We can take care of them there, and they'll be totally separate from the other animals here."

"That won't work." Kevin was frowning. "The virus is transmitted from dog to dog through the air. That means this whole kennel will need to be disinfected if we want to keep more animals from catching it."

"Wait, so we aren't going to move the sick dogs?" Jack asked. "We're going to move all the *other* dogs?"

"I'm afraid we have to," Kevin said. "This virus is far too dangerous to keep the other dogs here."

"And I have a litter of puppies here, too," Annie said. "They're not old enough for the vaccine. They won't make it if they get sick."

"There's no cure for distemper. The only way to deal with it is to treat the individual symptoms," Kevin told her. "That means treating the sick dogs for the seizures, the eye and nose discharge, the diarrhea and vomiting, and also for dehydration and possible breathing troubles. It's going to be a lot of work."

"I've got three employees who help me take care of all the animals that board here," Annie said. "All of us will stay and help you nurse the sickies."

"But then who's going to take care of the animals that aren't sick?" Jack asked. "And where are we going to send them?"

Kevin and Annie looked at each other helplessly. "We've got cages at Creature Comforts," Kevin said. "We could move them all there. But I don't know who would take care of them. My daughter and her friend are off in Los Angeles for the weekend, and they're the ones who do all the work around the office."

"Maybe we should call them back," Jack suggested.

Kevin just raised an eyebrow.

"Okay, okay, bad idea," Jack admitted. "But here's a brilliant idea: Send the animals to Victoria's ranch."

"Victoria? How would that help?" Kevin asked.

"It's perfect!" Jack said. "We'll bring the cages over there from Creature Comforts. Then Victoria and Eli can take care of all the animals. Victoria will totally want to help when she hears about the situation."

"That's true," Kevin said, turning to Annie. "Victoria is a big animal lover."

"And, you know, I can stay at the ranch to give them a hand," Jack added casually.

Kevin gazed at him for a moment, and Jack tried to keep an innocent look on his face. Sure, he was counting on Victoria to make him famous some day. And sure, he was always trying to score points with her. And sure, she would be impressed by his willingness to care for the poor, displaced pets. But that didn't mean the plan wasn't a good one for the animals, too.

"Okay," Kevin finally said. "I'll go call her. But I hope you know how much work you're in for, Jack."

Jack grinned. "I can't wait."

"Tru! You look amazing," Darcy exclaimed when she spotted her old friend near the potted cacti in the hotel lobby. "That dress is perfect."

"Thanks." Tru gave her a kiss on the cheek. Darcy noticed Lindsay and Kathi staring at her as if she'd gone crazy. Friends didn't kiss each other hello in Bailey the way they did here. She'd have to explain it to them later—or else they'd be surprised when Tru and

Riley started kissing *them* hello, too!

"I love your shoes," Tru said, checking out Darcy's wedge heels. "New?"

"Are you kidding? They're a year old," Darcy said. "There's no shoe shopping in Bailey. My mom doesn't give me an allowance. If I want something, I have to work for the money. So I go for jeans first, then purses, then jewelry, and then shoes."

Tru laughed. "So the shoes are all last season."

"I prefer to call them retro," Darcy said. "Did you see Andre?"

"He's outside with the car," Tru told her. "Should we go? He wants to take Mulholland Drive all the way out to the coast so your friends can see the views."

"That's a great idea," Darcy said, feeling a little ashamed that she hadn't thought of that herself. "You guys will get to see the whole city from up there."

Kathi froze halfway across the lobby. "Then I should go get the camcorder. I left it upstairs."

Tru's eyes widened. "You want to film the drive? Why?"

"Because it's pretty," Kathi replied.

"Yeah, but it would take forever to film the whole thing," Tru said. "You can just buy a couple of post-cards and get the best parts."

"Don't you have one of the still cameras with you?" Darcy asked. "Take pictures with that."

"Okay," Kathi said quietly.

Darcy could see that her friend was bummed about not getting the camcorder. But they were running late, and Tru was right—the photos on postcards were better than anything you could film on your own. She was sure Kathi would realize that once she got a good look at the view from the top of the hills. No video could ever do justice to the sight of Los Angeles gleaming down below, stretching out as far as the eye could see. Darcy led the way out to the short driveway in front of the hotel and waved to Andre. He jogged around the car and opened the back door for the girls. "Ladies," he said with a grin. "Ready for a big night out?"

"Not really," Kathi grumbled. "I don't have my video camera."

Andre laughed. "Maybe you'll have more fun looking at things directly instead of through a viewfinder."

Kathi gave him a small smile. "That's true," she admitted.

"You really don't have to open the car door for us, Andre," Lindsay said. "We can do it ourselves."

"It's my pleasure," Andre told her. "How else could I make sure I had you all safe inside?"

He ushered them into the limo and shut the door behind them. Darcy climbed across the seat to make room for Lindsay and Kathi to sit by the windows so they'd get the best views. "This is gonna be so much fun," she said. "We have the whole drive to just talk and catch up."

"I want to hear everything," Tru agreed. "What's the gossip from Bailey?"

Darcy, Kathi, and Lindsay stared at each other blankly. "Um . . . actually, there isn't any," Darcy said. "The biggest topic of conversation there lately is the *lack* of gossip. Nothing happens in August, apparently. No parties, no movies, no clients at the vet's office. Nothing."

"It's pretty boring," Lindsay agreed.

"Well, not always," Darcy said. "Usually there's lots of fun stuff going on. It's just this month that's been boring."

"Oh." Tru glanced at Darcy. "Well, are you dating anyone?"

"No," Darcy said. "How can I? All the available boys are on vacation!"

"Everybody goes away in August," Kathi explained. "And there aren't that many cute boys even when people are in town."

"Oh," Tru said again. She didn't seem to know what else to say. For a moment nobody spoke. Darcy glanced at her old friend and her new friends, willing them to find some common ground. They were all so cool and so much fun—how could they not get along? Sure, Bailey and Los Angeles were pretty different, but so what? If only her friends would get to know one another better, they'd love each other.

"Hey, Tru, did I ever tell you that Lindsay's favorite movie is *Gone With the Wind*?" Darcy asked. "Doesn't your dad have an original framed poster from that film in his office?"

"Yeah," Tru said. "I've never seen the movie, though."

"Oh." Darcy sighed. So much for that topic of conversation. She tried another one. "Kathi, Tru's older brother has a vintage car kinda like the one we saw on the freeway today. I bet your dad would love it." She turned to Tru. "Kathi's family owns a car dealership."

"What kind of car does your brother have?" Kathi asked.

Tru shrugged. "It's a Chevy, I think. I don't really like old cars. I never pay attention to him when he talks about it."

"Oh." Kathi looked a little embarrassed.

I can't stand to hear the word "oh" one more time, Darcy thought in despair. Why couldn't she get a conversation going between her friends?

"Check it out," Lindsay said suddenly. She pointed

out the window. "There are horses down there! Is that a ranch?"

"I think it's a riding stable," Darcy said, leaning forward to look. "People like to ride up here in the hills. There are horse trails with great views."

"Look at that one! It looks like Midnight from the Brennan brothers' place," Kathi said. "Remember when she stole that entire cookie from Eli just as he was about to bite into it?"

"That was hysterical," Darcy said. "Eli just chomped down on nothing but air!"

They all laughed at the memory. Poor Eli could never catch a break. "And Midnight whinnied at him as if she thought it was funny," Lindsay added.

"She probably did think it was funny. She *is* a retired circus horse," Darcy said. "I bet she learned a lot about comedy from the clowns."

"Remember that clown who brought her to the Brennans' in the first place?" Kathi said. "What was his name?"

"El Chubbo Magnifico," Lindsay replied. "Even though he was really skinny."

Darcy chuckled at the memory. But when she glanced over at Tru, she caught her old friend in the middle of a yawn. *Uh-oh,* she thought. *We're so busy talking about Bailey stuff that Tru probably feels left out.*

"What about you, Tru?" Darcy asked. "What's the gossip around here?"

Tru perked up a little. "Well, the best news is that Matt Boutry broke up with Lotus," she said.

"No!" Darcy gasped. "They've been dating since sixth grade!"

"I know," Tru said. "Lotus freaked out and didn't come to school for a week. Then she showed up with all her hair cut off."

"Is she . . . bald?" Darcy asked, scandalized.

"No, but it's practically a crew cut," Tru said with a giggle. "I think she's trying to look punk, but she can't pull it off."

"That is too funny," Darcy said. She shot a look at Kathi and Lindsay. "You have to know this girl Lotus. She's really prissy, so it's kinda out of character."

Lindsay just looked back at her without saying anything. Kathi smiled politely.

They don't care what happened to Lotus, Darcy thought. *They don't even know her!*

Darcy sighed, frustrated. What was she supposed to do? Tru didn't know anyone in Bailey, so she wouldn't want to talk about life back there. And Lindsay and Kathi didn't know anyone here in Los Angeles, so they didn't want to talk about life here.

One thing was for sure: It was going to be a long car ride.

"Eli! Careful with that parrot cage!" Jack called. "It's leaning a little to the left."

Eli glanced at the cage, which sat on top of two big dog crates in the back of Kevin's pickup truck. "It looks straight to me," he said.

"I'm telling you, it's ever so slightly off balance," Jack insisted. "Oh, and you need to move Pucci away from Dodger. Annie says they don't get along."

Eli pushed his longish hair out of his eyes and sighed. "I just got them both loaded. They can get along for the ten-minute ride from here to the ranch. They're not even in the same crate."

"But they're next to each other," Jack said. "They can *see* each other. Do you want to be responsible for vicious barking all the way along the ride?"

"Jack," Victoria said, coming out of McCormick's McBoardinghouse with a cat carrier. "I think you could help us more by carrying out some of the animals. Pucci and Dodger are fine where they are. And we have at least ten more animals to load, and then we'll have to make another trip."

"If not two trips," Eli put in. "There are a lot of animals. We took all the cages and crates from Creature

Comforts, but I don't think there will be e

"Then some of the larger dogs can go

horse stalls in the barn at the ranch," Vic

"I'm certainly happy to help out in a crisis like this,

but I'm afraid it's going to be quite a lot of work."

"Don't you worry," Jack told her. "You're not in

this alone. Whatever you need, I'll do it. I'm your

number one guy, your right-hand man."

"Good. Then I need you to help load the animals

onto the pickup," Victoria said.

"I am helping. I'm supervising the loading," Jack

pointed out.

Victoria raised her perfectly-groomed eyebrows.

"Supervising?"

"That's right."

"Tell you what. Eli and I will supervise ourselves,

and then you'll be free to carry some animals out,"

Victoria said.

Jack opened his mouth, but he couldn't think of a

good argument.

"Great. It's settled." Victoria smiled. "There are

two iguanas in there. They need to be put into carrying

cases and brought out here. I think they'll have to ride

on our laps in the cab."

"Iguanas?" Jack asked. "People actually leave

iguanas at kennels?"

"There are also a couple of chinchillas and a boa constrictor," Eli said.

"Nobody wants their pet to get lonely when they go away, no matter what kind of pet it is," Victoria said. "And since Annie and her staff will be busy helping Kevin care for the sick dogs, it's up to the three of us to make sure all these beloved pets are happy and well taken care of." She looked back and forth between Eli and Jack. "It's going to be a fun weekend, boys!"

Chapter 5

"These are the best blueberry pancakes I've ever had!" Lindsay said on Saturday morning.

"Actually, they're blueberry-blackberry pancakes," Darcy corrected her. "The blackberry is what gives them that little kick."

"Is there anything in Los Angeles that's just plain old normal?" Lindsay asked. "I mean, even the food at that restaurant last night wasn't normal. All sushi and seafood, no burgers or anything. Their most normal fish was octopus!"

"I can't believe you ate that," Kathi said.

"It was really good, actually," Lindsay replied.

"Well, I like the not-normal," Kathi said. "Eating breakfast by the pool at a swanky hotel isn't normal—and I love it!"

Darcy leaned back in her chair and let the sun shine on her face. "Mmm, I've missed the not-normal California cuisine," she said. "Believe me, living on a diet of Eli's food is truly not normal. The boy can cook, but every meal is accompanied by some kind of disaster!" She checked her watch. An hour until they had to meet Riley and Tru for their big spa day. Darcy couldn't wait to see the looks on her Bailey friends' faces when she told them about it!

"Guess what?" she said.

"Is that somebody famous?" Kathi asked suddenly. "On the other side of the pool, with the blue shirt on?"

Darcy squinted over at the guy with the blue shirt. "I don't think so. So, listen . . ."

"He looks just like that guy from that show," Lindsay said. "The one with the radio station where they all work."

"Yeah!" Kathi agreed. "I think it is him."

"Maybe it's his stunt double," Darcy said. "Anyway—"

"Do stunt doubles really look that much like the real actors?" Kathi asked. "That's weird."

"I guess." Darcy felt like she was about to burst. She hurried on before Kathi could ask any more questions. "I've got the best surprise for you two!"

"What is it?" Lindsay asked.

"Guess what we're doing today?" Darcy couldn't help bouncing up and down a little in her excitement to tell them the news. "Spa day!"

Her friends didn't answer.

"Spa day," Darcy repeated. "At Georgette Klinger in Beverly Hills. The best place in the whole city!"

"Wow. Beverly Hills," Kathi said. "Isn't that expensive?"

"Yeah, but it's my treat," Darcy told her. "Well, it's my mom's treat. She knows how much I love that place. I couldn't come home and not go there."

"So we're going for the whole day?" Lindsay asked slowly. "What do you do at a spa for a whole day?"

"We're starting with manicures and pedicures," Darcy said. "Tru and Riley are meeting us there in an hour—we booked five manicure stations all together. Then we all get facials. Then we have the spa lunch. It's incredibly yummy. And then in the afternoon there are massages and hanging out in the hot tub."

"Massages?" Kathi asked nervously. "I don't think I want some stranger touching my back."

"Don't worry, they're professionals," Darcy assured her. "It's totally relaxing. They play New Age music and there's aromatherapy and everything. I can practically smell the ylang-ylang already!"

Lindsay looked at Kathi, then back at Darcy. "Um,

that's really generous of your mom, Darcy," she said. "Did she already pay for all that stuff?"

"No, she gave me a credit card to use," Darcy replied. "Why?"

"Well, it's just . . . kind of not my thing," Lindsay said. "You know I don't like all that pampering stuff. I never even do my own nails."

"Yeah, and besides, it seems like it will take up the entire day," Kathi added.

"That's why they call it a spa *day*," Darcy said.

"I know. But we only have today and tomorrow," Kathi said. "I just assumed that we would go sightseeing today. Are we doing that tomorrow instead?"

Darcy's smile froze. This wasn't the reaction she'd been expecting. "Sightseeing," she repeated. "Uh . . . I hadn't really thought about it. What sights did you want to see?"

"Well, there's Grauman's Chinese Theatre," Kathi said. "Where all the stars put their footprints in the concrete, right?"

"And there's the Walk of Fame, with a star for each famous person," Lindsay added. "The website I visited said those things are both in the same place."

"And then I want to see the Hollywood sign and the theater where they present the Oscars," Kathi rushed on. "And there's a museum for the Ripley's Believe It or Not stuff . . ."

Darcy's heart sank. She knew where all those places were, of course. But she'd never paid much attention to them before. Grauman's Chinese Theatre was just a place where you went to see movies. And the Walk of Fame was . . . well, it was just a sidewalk.

". . . and then there's Rodeo Drive," Kathi was saying. "Even though I could never afford to buy anything there."

"Actually, Rodeo Drive isn't really that swanky anymore," Darcy told her. "It's just the same stores you see in the mall."

"It's not the stores, it's the people," Kathi said. "I bet we could see movie stars shopping there."

"Linds?" Darcy asked. "Do you want to see all that stuff, too?"

"Not really," Lindsay said. "But the websites I looked at all said that Griffith Park has some of the best hiking trails in the city. And we could hike almost all the way up to the Hollywood sign."

"Hiking?" Darcy asked. "Seriously? You want to go hiking?" Even her mother had laughed at her for thinking she might go hiking during a weekend trip to L.A.

"Yeah. Don't you?" Lindsay asked.

Darcy didn't know what to say. Between schlepping around to a bunch of tourist traps, hiking in the middle of nowhere, and having a luxurious day of pampering at her favorite spa . . . well, it was a no-brainer. "I wasn't really planning to go hiking," she said. "I sort of assumed we'd hang out with my old friends and do the stuff I normally did when I lived here."

"But you must've spent a lot of time shopping on Rodeo Drive, right?" Kathi asked. "And hanging out on the Walk of Fame?"

"Rodeo Drive, sure," Darcy said with a laugh. "My mom would say I spent way too much time there. But the Walk of Fame isn't really where you hang out. It's mostly for tourists. I mean, it's really crowded all the time, and there are all kinds of tacky little T-shirt shops all along there."

Lindsay sighed. "I keep forgetting that we're not supposed to be *tourists*," she said.

"That's not what I meant," Darcy replied. "It's just that I'm not a tourist. When you live in a place, you think about it differently, I guess. I didn't realize that you guys would want to do all that stuff."

"Well, we didn't realize you would want to spend all day at a spa," Kathi said. "We probably should have planned this trip better."

"And I shouldn't have tried to surprise you with a spa day you don't want," Darcy said. The massages at Georgette Klinger were calling to her, but she couldn't very well force her friends to get spa treatments that would make them miserable. And so far, she'd barely even seen Lindsay smile during this trip. "Tell you what," Darcy said. "We'll hike this morning and see the sights this afternoon. That way you both get to do what you want."

"But Darcy, then you won't get to do what you want," Lindsay said. "What about the spa?"

"We won't go."

"But won't your mom have to pay for the appointments anyway?" Lindsay asked, concerned.

"Nah," Darcy said. "The spa will give her a credit to use whenever she's in town again."

"But what about your friends?" Kathi put in. "You said we're supposed to meet them in an hour."

"I'll just have to call and cancel," Darcy said. She reached for her cell phone, and hesitated. If she called Tru, Tru would be bummed. And that would make Darcy feel bummed. And Lindsay and Kathi would be sure to hear the disappointment in her voice, even if she managed to keep it off her face. "Or maybe I'll wait until we get back upstairs and just IM them," she said. That way, maybe she could keep all of her friends from realizing how upset she really was.

Darcy: Hey.

TruBlue: Whazup? I'm already on my way to GK.

Can't wait for my mani/pedi! Where R U?

Darcy1: At the hotel.

TruBlue: You're gonna be late.

Darcy1: Bad news. Can't do the spa day.

TruBlue: What??? Why???

Darcy1: Lindsay wants to hike and Kathi wants to go to the Hollywood Strip.

TruBlue: Instead of the spa? Why???

Darcy1: They're just not into the spa. They want to see L.A.

Darcy1: You still there?

Darcy1: Hello?

TruBlue: Yeah. But we're supposed to spend the whole day together. I miss you.

Darcy1: I miss you guys, too. Sorry.

TruBlue: This stinks.

Darcy1: I know. Have fun at the spa. I'm jealous. :(

TruBlue: :(too. L8R.

"I can't believe my mother talked me out of bringing hiking boots," Darcy said, staring up the steep hill of Runyon Canyon.

"I only have sneakers, too," Kathi said. "Don't worry—we'll just make Lindsay pull us up the hard parts."

"You wish!" Lindsay laughed. "That trail goes straight uphill."

"I can't believe how crowded it is here," Kathi said. "This place is packed."

"Yup. This is the most popular hiking spot," Darcy told her. "It's where all the stars go. I figured we might get to see someone famous for Kathi and we'll still get a good hike in for Lindsay."

"Cool. Thanks, Darce." Lindsay charged up to the trailhead, her cheeks flushed and her eyes sparkling.

Darcy followed, glad to see her friend looking happy for a change. By the time they'd been hiking for half an hour, Lindsay was about twenty feet in front of them.

"She's practically jogging up this hill," Kathi panted.

"I know." Darcy took a long gulp of her bottled water. "She's having fun."

"Well, I have to rest," Kathi said. "And take some pictures. Let me get one of you with the view of the city behind you."

Darcy went over to the edge of the trail and held out her arms like a game-show hostess demonstrating the grand prize. "Can you see the buildings behind me?"

"Kind of," Kathi said, peering into the viewfinder of her camera. "Say cheese."

"Brie!" Darcy sang, putting on a big smile.

"Beautiful," said a deep voice. "Let me take one of both of you." A tall guy with curly blond hair stood behind Kathi, looking over her shoulder. Kathi jumped, but Darcy gasped in surprise.

"Caleb?" she cried.

"Hey, Darce." The guy grinned, a dimple appearing in each cheek.

Darcy rushed over and threw her arms around him, getting tangled in a dog leash he held in his hand. "Sorry," he said. "Buster's still a puppy. He doesn't get the whole concept of 'heel' yet."

Darcy bent down to pat the young German shepherd on his head, then looked back up at Caleb. "You're about a foot taller than last time I saw you."

He nodded. "Well, it's been a while. I heard you moved to Idaho or something."

"Not quite. But something like that," Darcy told him. "This is my friend Kathi. She's from Bailey, where I live now."

"Hi, Kathi. That's a great camera," Caleb said.

"Thanks." Kathi was blushing furiously, and Darcy hid a grin. She'd known Caleb since fifth grade, but even she had to admit he'd gotten majorly cute.

"Kath, this is Caleb. His mother was the director of my mom's movie *Love Talks*," Darcy introduced him.

"I adore that movie," Kathi said. "It played in town for about three months when it came out, and I saw it five times."

"Wow." Caleb glanced at Darcy.

"There's only one movie theater," she explained. "And films tend to stick around for a while. You pretty much see every movie there a couple of times because there's nothing else to do."

"Sounds brutal," Caleb said.

"Not so much," Darcy told him. "It's kind of nice, actually. Here everybody acts as if movies are the most important thing in the world. But in Bailey they're just movies."

"Are you guys coming?" Lindsay called down. She was way ahead of them, about twenty feet higher up the steep hill.

"Coming!" Darcy called back. "This hill is what's brutal," she joked to Caleb. "I'd forgotten how steep Runyon Canyon is. Not that I ever really hiked it before. I used to just come sit at the bottom near the trailhead and pretend I'd finished hiking up and back down."

"Why would you do that?" Kathi asked as they started slowly along the trail.

"Because it's *the* place to be seen," Caleb answered for Darcy. "All the big stars and directors and producers hike here."

"You mean I could be discovered right here?" Kathi giggled. "Right now?"

"It's a possibility," Darcy said. "But what with the actual hiking and all, neither of us is gonna look pretty enough to be discovered today!"

"I don't know about that," Caleb said. "You still look pretty good to me, Darce."

Her cheeks heated up, and she hoped he thought it was from the exertion of climbing the hill.

"Do you have a boyfriend back in Bailey?" Caleb asked.

"Well, there is this one guy," Darcy said. "He's super-adorable. Dark hair, big, sweet brown eyes. He doesn't say much, but I can tell he loves me."

"Oh." Caleb looked disappointed.

"Yeah, his name is Gus," Darcy went on. "He's a horse."

"What does that mean?" Caleb asked, confused. "He's strong?"

"No, it means he's a horse," Kathi put in. "With

four legs and a tail. He lives on Darcy's ranch."

Caleb laughed. "I don't know if I can compete with that," he said.

"It's about time," Lindsay said as they approached. She was sitting on a big boulder at a curve in the trail. Buster went bounding up and licked her face.

"Sorry," Darcy said. "We didn't mean to keep you waiting."

"I'm just kidding. I've been having the best time," Lindsay replied. "There are so many dogs here! I got to pet every one as it came by. Just like this one." She rubbed Buster between the ears.

"This is dog central," Caleb agreed. "People make doggie playdates to bring their pooches hiking up the canyon."

"Lindsay, this is Caleb," Darcy said. "Lindsay's another Bailey friend."

"Hey," Caleb greeted her. "So, are you girls just in for the weekend?"

Darcy nodded. "Things are pretty slow at home these days, so my mom sent us here for some fun."

"How is Victoria?" Caleb asked. "And when are you two moving back to civilization? I figured your mother would be bored by now out there in the middle of nowhere."

"Hey!" Lindsay protested. "Just because Bailey slows

down in the summertime doesn't mean it's nowheres-ville."

"Oh, sorry." Caleb winced. "I didn't mean any offense. It's just that Darcy's mom had such a busy lifestyle here, with all the parties and premieres."

"She doesn't miss it," Darcy said with a sigh. "She's totally happy on the ranch."

"And how about you?" Caleb asked.

"I like Bailey," Darcy replied. "But now that I'm back in L.A., it still feels like home. A little."

"Omigosh!" Kathi suddenly squealed. Then she clapped her hand over her mouth. "Sorry, Darcy," she said, her voice muffled by her fingers.

"What's wrong?" Darcy asked, concerned.

Kathi pulled her hand away and dropped her voice. "I didn't mean to scream so loud. But I think that woman who just walked past us is Julia Roberts!"

They all turned to look. All Darcy could see was a reddish-brown ponytail bobbing as the woman walked.

"Let's follow her and get close enough to see for sure," Caleb said with a mischievous smile. "Come on, Buster!"

They all took off after the woman, trying to look casual.

"I can't get the camera to focus right while I'm walking," Kathi complained, fiddling with the lens.

Then she glanced at Darcy. "Is it okay if I take a picture of her? I don't want to embarrass you again."

Darcy felt a little stab in her heart. She'd made Kathi totally paranoid with that thing about Dylan Strong yesterday. "Of course it's okay," she told her friend. "You do whatever you want."

Kathi immediately put the camera back up to her face and began snapping photos of the woman's back.

"Just don't walk off the edge of the cliff," Darcy added quickly, grabbing Kathi's arm.

"Want me to jog up there with Buster and see if it's her?" Caleb asked. "She likes dogs, I hear."

"No, that's okay," Kathi said with a smile at Darcy. "I don't want to bother her. Just seeing a big star is all I needed to make the whole trip perfect!"

SmileyRiley: Hey, Darce.

Darcy: Hi, Ri. How's GK? Did you have the delish spa lunch yet?

SmileyRiley: Not yet. Tru's still finishing up her facial.

Darcy: I'm so bummed I can't be there.

SmileyRiley: You hiking?

Darcy1: Yup. Runyon Canyon. We went all the way to the top. Resting before we go back down.

SmileyRiley: Ouch!

Darcy1: I know! Caleb's here.

SmileyRiley: Ooh.

Darcy1: He got cute.

SmileyRiley: :)

SmileyRiley: Friends having fun?

Darcy1: Seems like it.

SmileyRiley: Good.

Darcy1: L8R we're going sightseeing.

SmileyRiley: Where?

Darcy1: Hollywoodish. Wherever Kathi & Lindsay want.

SmileyRiley: OK. Wanna meet for lunch?

Darcy1: At GK?

SmileyRiley: No. We'll come to you.

Darcy1: What about spa lunch?

SmileyRiley: Change in plans. We're gonna skip the massages and come with you.

Darcy1: Wha???

SmileyRiley: See the sights like tourists. :)

Darcy1: Seriously?

SmileyRiley: Could be fun. B-sides, we miss you.

Darcy1: OMG, that would be SOOOOOOO great!

SmileyRiley: Meet you at the hotel in an hour?

Darcy1: See you then.

Darcy1: Yay! We're gonna have the best afternoon!

Chapter 6

Wild Wisdom . . . *Parrots raised by humans have an incredible ability to mimic people and noisy objects, but in the wild parrots have never been observed mimicking.*

"I am exhausted," Jack complained, throwing himself into one of the dining room chairs at Victoria's ranch. "And hungry. What's for lunch, Eli?"

Eli lifted his head from the table, where he'd been resting it. "Lunch?" he asked, his brown eyes filled with dismay.

"Don't worry, Eli. Nobody expects you to make lunch today," Victoria said from her seat. "We'll all pitch in and do something easy, like tuna. Or better yet, cereal. No preparation needed." She went into the kitchen and came back with a few boxes of cereal and some milk, while Eli grabbed bowls and spoons.

Jack stayed where he was. He glanced around at all the cages and crates scattered about the house. Most of the dogs and cats were sleeping, which looked pretty good to him. He yawned. "Do we have time for a siesta?"

he asked. "Feeding all those animals was hard work! I knew the snake had weird eating habits, but who knew dogs and cats could be such picky eaters? At least half of them are on special diets."

"Annie certainly has a lot to keep track of when she's boarding this many pets," Victoria agreed. "I thought Darcy was finicky about her food! But Mr. Orrin's Labradoodles wouldn't eat anything but grilled chicken—and only if I sat next to their cage and fed it to them by hand!"

"That's nothing," Eli said, chomping on some shredded wheat. "The parrot's cage is in the kitchen, and he kept heckling me while I was trying to get all the other animals' food ready."

"Well, I'm glad morning feeding is over," Jack said. "Even if it did take us until one o'clock in the afternoon! Now we can relax until it's time for evening feeding."

"Sorry. I'm afraid we can't." Victoria poured milk over her cereal. "All the dogs need to get some exercise before we feed them again."

Jack's mouth fell open. "All of them? Why?"

"Because that's part of what Annie promises their owners when they leave their pets with her. Dogs need walks. They can't stay in their cages all day long."

"Well, sure, they need to go out and do their

business," Jack said. "But that just means a five-minute walk, right? And we can take a bunch of dogs at a time."

"No, Jack, they don't just need a quick walk," Victoria told him. "Annie promises half an hour of exercise a day. And she also promises that each dog will be exercised alone."

Jack's mouth fell open. "But why?"

"Because dogs don't always get along," Victoria said. "And if two of them get into a fight and hurt each other, Annie will be responsible for it. So the dogs have to be kept separate unless the owner has given permission for them to play with another dog."

Jack thought about it. There were at least twelve dogs in the house. Half an hour each would be six hours' worth of exercising. "When are we supposed to start the evening feeding?" he asked.

"In four hours," Victoria said.

"Plus we need to clean out all the cages and wash all the bedding," Eli added. "And not only for the dogs— for the cats, too. And I guess for the chinchillas."

"And for Beaker, the parrot," Victoria continued.

"In four hours?" Jack exclaimed, incredulously. "But just exercising the dogs is going to take six hours!"

"So you can see our problem," Victoria said.

"How do Annie and her workers do all that?" Jack sputtered. "It's . . . it's impossible!"

"Well, it *is* their full-time job," Victoria pointed out.

"But we can't do that. This is an emergency situation," Jack cried. "These animals are refugees!"

"They're still entitled to the best care we can give them," Victoria said firmly. "We're going to do everything that Annie promised their owners. We're just going to have to be a bit creative about it."

Jack wasn't sure that he liked the sound of that. "Meaning what?" he asked.

Victoria pushed back her chair and stood up. "Follow me, boys," she said. "We'll start with Rocky here." She opened the door of a large cage that had been set up in the living room, clipped a leash to the collar of the rottweiler inside, and led him out of the house.

Eli went right after her, but Jack stopped to grab an apple for the walk. By the time he caught up with them, Victoria, Eli, and Rocky were out by the old horseback-riding ring behind the ranch house.

"It's the perfect size," Victoria was saying. "We'll set up an assembly line from the house to here. I'll go in and get each dog, then I'll bring them out here. Eli, you'll exercise them."

"But it will still take too long," Eli said. "If each one is out here for half an hour, we'll be here all afternoon!"

"Yes, well . . ." Victoria bit her lip. "There is one

95

catch. We simply don't have the time to give each dog its full half hour. So I think you're going to have to jog with the dogs instead of walking them."

"Jog," Eli repeated, beginning to sound alarmed.

"Yes. A ten-minute jog has to be just as good as a half-hour walk, right?" Victoria said brightly.

"So I'm going to jog with each dog around the riding ring for ten minutes," Eli said.

"Exactly. Then by the time you're done running with one, I'll be back out with the next one," Victoria said. "I'll take the one you've finished with, and you'll take the new one and start jogging again. See? It's an assembly line."

"Okay," Eli said. "That will work." He took Rocky's leash, led him into the ring, and began jogging. The big dog loped happily along next to him, his tongue hanging out.

"There's just one problem," Jack said as he and Victoria began walking back to the house. "What am I supposed to do in this assembly line?"

"Oh, the most important job of all," she replied. "While Eli is jogging with the dog, you'll be cleaning out its cage."

Jack stopped chewing his apple. "You mean—"

"That's right, clean up any accidents the dog has had and scrub each cage so that it's absolutely sterile,"

Victoria chirped. "But you have to do it fast—you only have ten minutes!"

"But . . . but . . . how about I bring the dogs in and out?" Jack said, desperation creeping into his voice.

"You aren't suggesting that *I* clean out the cages?" Victoria asked archly.

Jack sighed. He couldn't very well stay on Victoria's good side if he asked her to pick up dog poop. "No, I'll do it," he mumbled, heading for the kitchen to get the cleaning supplies.

This impress-Victoria plan was getting worse by the minute!

"Hey, girls!" Darcy cried when she spotted Riley and Tru on the couches in the lobby. "You look so relaxed." She rushed over to kiss them hello, while Kathi and Lindsay followed more slowly.

"Like my mani?" Tru held out her hand to show off bright turquoise nail polish.

"It's hideous," Darcy told her. "Is that in style now?"

Riley laughed. "No, Tru's just trying to make it be in style."

"What can I say? I'm on a turquoise kick lately," Tru said. "My toes match, see?"

Darcy glanced down at her friend's leather-and-beadwork flip-flops and bright blue toes. "Wow," she said. "You look great. My poor toes are so sad compared to yours. I haven't had a real pedicure in months."

"Sorry, Darcy," Kathi said. "You could've gotten one this morning if not for us."

"That's not what I meant," Darcy insisted. "I'm just saying . . . my toes look ugly." It sounded lame, but she didn't know what else to say. She hadn't wanted to make her Bailey friends feel guilty. But she *was* kind of jealous of Tru's pedicure.

"Ready to go?" Riley asked. "I'm starving."

"Me too," Lindsay said. "Hiking all morning is hard work."

"Oh. I guess going to the spa doesn't really compare," Riley said. Darcy waited for her to laugh or say she was kidding, but she didn't.

There was an awkward silence, and Lindsay looked a little offended. "I wouldn't know. I've never been to one," she said.

"Hey, is that Duchess?" Darcy asked, grabbing for Riley's purse. "I thought I saw a little nose sticking out of there!" She pulled the tiny Chihuahua from the bag and gave her a kiss, hoping the dog would distract her friends. There was a weird vibe going on between Lindsay and Riley.

"Ooh, how adorable!" Kathi cooed, petting Duchess. "Look at her little rhinestone collar."

"You keep a dog in your purse?" Lindsay asked, eyebrows raised.

"Yeah. She goes everywhere with me," Riley said, leaning over to kiss the dog on her little head.

"But in a purse?" Lindsay asked. "Don't you think it's a little cramped in there?"

"No," Riley said with a frown.

"Not for a dog as itty-bitty as Duchess," Darcy weighed in. "And not with a purse as big as that. Where did you get it, by the way?"

It worked. Riley's frown vanished. "At this great new place on Melrose," she said. "They have it in six different colors."

"Ladies," Andre called from the doorway. "Ready whenever you are."

"Great." Darcy grabbed Lindsay's arm and pulled her toward the door, wanting to keep her as far from Riley as possible. When they got into the limo, she made sure the two girls were sitting as far apart as she could get them.

"So, where are we having lunch?" Tru asked. "The Ivy? Dolce?"

"Um, no," Darcy said, her cheeks heating up a little. "We're just going up the street to House of Blues."

"Really?" Tru asked. "But that's—"

99

"Totally within walking distance, I know," Darcy interrupted her. She knew her friend had been about to say the place was a tourist trap, but she didn't want Kathi to hear that. Ignoring Tru's confused frown, she rushed on. "But I'm so exhausted from the hike, I can't bear the thought of walking another step right now."

She kept up a constant stream of talk until they reached the restaurant, but she couldn't help noticing that none of her friends had much to say. Tru and Riley talked to each other, and Kathi and Lindsay talked to each other. And they all talked to Darcy.

But not to one another.

All through lunch, Darcy felt like a referee trying to negotiate between her friends. Kathi wanted to share an onion loaf for the appetizer, but Tru refused to eat anything fried. And since Riley was a vegetarian, she freaked out when Lindsay ordered a big hamburger for her main course. Tru and Riley wanted mango sorbet for dessert, and they couldn't understand why the girls from Bailey preferred ice-cream sundaes.

By the time the check came, Darcy was exhausted. She'd always thought she was good at small talk, but doing nothing else for an hour was really hard.

"I think I'm going to buy a House of Blues T-shirt on the way out," Kathi said while they waited to pay. "This place is great."

Tru glanced around and shrugged. "It's okay. My salad was actually pretty good."

"Yeah, I was surprised," Riley agreed. "I figured the food would stink."

"Haven't you ever eaten here before?" Lindsay asked, surprised.

"Nope," Tru said. "I came to a charity-benefit party here once, but that was at night, and they served hors d'oeuvres only. None of their regular menu food."

"Wow," Kathi said. "If I lived in L.A., I would eat here every day!"

Tru shrugged. "It's too much of a tourist trap for me."

Darcy felt the blood drain from her face. She'd managed to avoid the whole "tourist" thing all through lunch, but somehow it had still come out. She saw Kathi's happy expression disappear, replaced by one of embarrassment. Tru was oblivious, of course. She hadn't realized that her comment sounded insulting to Kathi.

What am I supposed to say? Darcy thought frantically. She didn't want Kathi to feel stupid, but she also didn't want to make Tru feel bad. The place *was* kind of a tourist trap, after all. And Tru hadn't intended to put Kathi down. "Um . . . sightseeing?" she said, pasting a smile on her face.

"Is that going to be too boring for you guys?" Kathi asked quietly. "I know it's kind of touristy, too."

"No way," Darcy replied. "As long as we're all together, we'll have fun doing anything. Right, Tru?"

"Sure," Tru said.

"Okay." Darcy took a deep breath. Balancing old and new friends wasn't easy! "Let's go get Andre and head for the Walk of Fame."

"So then Ms. Munoz tells Jess to go to the locker room and wash it off. And Jess has to admit it's an actual tattoo!" Riley said.

Darcy's eyes widened as she took another sip of her soy latte.

"And Ms. Munoz called her mom. Jess got in huge trouble," Tru added.

"I can't believe she got a tattoo," Darcy said. "My mother would kill me."

"You know Jess," Riley said. "She always has to take things too far."

Darcy sat back in the metal chair and glanced around the courtyard of the Hollywood & Highland Mall. "I've really missed a lot. Jess used to be so normal."

Tru shrugged. "She's always trying to impress Braden. He thinks he's such a wild child."

"Braden used to be normal, too," Darcy said. What

was going on with her old school friends? Tru and Riley had been telling her the gossip ever since they got to the mall half an hour ago, and Darcy couldn't believe her ears. Had she really been gone so long that everyone she knew had turned into someone else?

"Where's your friend Lindsay?" Tru asked suddenly. "Wasn't she just right here?"

Riley shook her head. "She took off ten minutes ago. I think she went to find Kathi."

Darcy bit her lip. "I didn't even notice that. I guess listening to us talk about people she doesn't know is pretty boring."

"So she can help Kathi find good stars on the ground to take pictures of," Riley said. "Somebody needs to keep the sidewalk clear so she can get the photos!"

Darcy chuckled. The Walk of Fame ran along the sidewalk of Hollywood Boulevard. It was right outside the mall—they could see a portion of it from their table in the open-air courtyard. Each black-speckled sidewalk square held a pink star with somebody's name on it. There were movie stars, directors, musicians, TV actors, and Broadway performers. The famous sidewalk ran for several blocks, and Kathi had wanted to take pictures of almost every star. Finally they'd decided to leave her to it while they got something to drink.

"How many stars do you think she's gotten by now?" Tru asked.

"I don't even know how many there are," Darcy admitted. "I never paid attention to them before. I just walked all over them!"

"Me too." Riley giggled. "And I never put my hands in the handprints at Grauman's Chinese Theatre before, either. That was kind of fun."

"I can't believe how small Sylvester Stallone's feet are! My feet are, like, three sizes bigger," Tru said.

Darcy felt herself relax a little. She'd been afraid her L.A. friends would hate all the sightseeing Kathi wanted to do. But maybe they hadn't thought it was so awful after all.

"Isn't it weird how you can live in a place your whole life and not even notice what all the tourists notice?" Tru asked.

"Yeah, and how you can live there and never appreciate the basic things, like soy lattes." Darcy took another sip of her latte, relishing the deliciousness of it. "You can't get these in Bailey."

"How can you stand it?" Riley asked. "Aren't you bored there?"

"Nope," Darcy said. "I thought I would be at first, but then it kinda grew on me. I mean, there are no premieres and there's no shopping and there are definitely no lattes. But the air is really clean, and the land is beautiful, and the people are totally nice."

"It still sounds boring," Tru said.

"Well, it has been boring lately," Darcy admitted. "But usually there's stuff going on. And there are always animals to take care of. I love working at the vet's office."

Tru and Riley exchanged a glance. "You love working?" Tru said skeptically.

"I know, it's weird." Darcy grinned. "Maybe I've changed as much as everyone here has."

"Hey, there's Kathi and Lindsay." Riley pointed to the wide stairway that led from the Walk of Fame up to the courtyard where they were sitting. Darcy's Bailey friends were snapping a photo of the star at the very bottom of it. "Should we go down?"

"Sure. I'm done with my drink." Darcy stood up and swung her purse strap onto her shoulder. Riley was more careful with her bag, since Duchess was inside. They all headed down the shallow stairs toward Lindsay and Kathi.

"Hey, Darce! I got a picture of Lucille Ball's star for my mom," Kathi called. "She loves Lucy."

"Cool," Darcy said.

"And then I made Lindsay pose with a guy dressed up as Spider-Man," Kathi went on. "How funny is that?"

"Not very," Lindsay grumbled, blushing. Darcy hid a smile. Lindsay hated to be the center of attention. She was surprised Lindsay had even agreed to pose for the picture.

"Are you done with the Walk of Fame?" Darcy asked.

"I think so," Kathi said. "Can we hit the Hollywood Wax Museum next? It's just around the corner."

"Well . . ." Darcy glanced at Tru and Riley to see how they felt about it. She didn't want to force them into more sightseeing than they could handle.

"Sounds good to me," Riley said. "Let's go."

"Don't you think you should give your dog some water first?" Lindsay asked. "She's panting a lot."

Darcy glanced at Duchess, whose tiny head was peeking out of Riley's purse. The Chihuahua really was panting heavily.

"Duchess!" Riley gasped. "Hang on, sweetie." She scurried over toward one of the stores lining Hollywood Boulevard, trying to get away from the stream of people walking by. Then she quickly knelt down and took Duchess out of her bag. The little dog stood on the sidewalk, her sides heaving as she panted.

"Poor baby," Darcy cooed, kneeling down to pet the dog. "Are you hot?"

Riley pulled a bottle of water and a tiny collapsible

bowl from her purse. She poured the water and put the bowl in front of Duchess. The Chihuahua lapped it up eagerly.

"Wow, she's really thirsty," Lindsay commented. "Did you just forget to give her any water today?"

Riley's eyes flashed with anger as she looked up at Lindsay. "No. I gave her a bowl of water twenty minutes ago," she snapped.

"Then why is she so thirsty?" Lindsay asked. Her tone seemed to say that she didn't believe Riley.

"Linds, I saw Duchess drink water not that long ago," Darcy affirmed. "She's probably just overheated."

"Well, she should stay out of the bag until she cools down," Lindsay said. "It's obviously way too hot in that purse for Duchess. I mean, it's hot out here. It's got to be even worse inside a cramped little bag."

"What's that supposed to mean?" Riley demanded.

"Just that maybe you should let your dog walk around on her own instead of keeping her trapped in a pocketbook," Lindsay said. "Let her get a little exercise for a change."

Riley stood up and stared Lindsay right in the eye. "Duchess runs all over the backyard when she's at home. She gets plenty of exercise."

"I haven't seen her get any today," Lindsay retorted. "All I see is an overheated dog who's thirsty."

"You don't know what you're talking about!" Riley snapped. "Everybody in Los Angeles carries their dogs around in their purses. Nobody has a problem with it except you."

"Then people in Los Angeles should be ashamed of themselves," Lindsay said. "It's cruel to keep a dog in a cramped, hot place and not give it any time to run around."

"You guys, stop arguing," Darcy begged, stepping in between them. "This is just a big misunderstanding—"

"Don't take her side," Riley interrupted. "You know it's completely normal for a Chihuahua to ride around in a purse."

"Well, that's true, Lindsay," Darcy said, turning to her friend. "Tons of small dogs live like this here. It's a totally acceptable life for them in L.A."

"That doesn't make it right," Lindsay said. "There are lots of stupid things in Los Angeles. Carrying a dog around until it gets overheated and sick is a dumb thing to do."

"How dare you call me dumb?" Riley cried.

"That's not what she meant," Darcy told Riley. "Lindsay's father is a veterinarian. She knows what she's talking about. Maybe it is too hot out today—"

"I can't believe you!" Riley cried. "You know I would never do anything to hurt Duchess."

"It's true, Lindsay, she wouldn't," Darcy said. "I think—"

"I don't care what you think," Lindsay cut in. "You're obviously going to side with Riley no matter what I say."

"No, I'm not," Darcy said.

"Thanks a lot, Darcy," Riley snapped. "You know what? I've had enough of this. I'm going home." She scooped up Duchess and stalked off, leaving the water bowl behind.

Darcy stared after her, horrified. What was she supposed to do now?

"Um, I think I better go with her," Tru said awkwardly. She snatched up Duchess's bowl. "Sorry, Darce." She hurried after Riley.

"Let's go," Lindsay muttered. She took off in the opposite direction.

"Wait! The Wax Museum is that way," Kathi called after her.

Lindsay stopped and whirled around to face them. She frowned at Darcy. "I'm not in the mood for any more Hollywood," she said coldly. "I just want to go back to the hotel." She stormed off toward the parking garage where Andre had left the car.

Kathi shot Darcy a sympathetic look, then followed Lindsay.

What just happened? Darcy thought miserably. *How could two people I like so much hate each other so much?*

Slowly she walked after her friends. So much for their big day of sightseeing.

Chapter 7

Wild Wisdom . . . *A camel can drink up to thirty gallons of water in just ten minutes!*

TruBlue: Wow. Pretty heavy stuff yesterday. You okay?

Darcy1: Sorta. Not sure what to do. I just wanted everyone to get along and have fun this weekend!

TruBlue: Is Lindsay mad?

Darcy1: Yup. She barely even talked to me at dinner last night.

TruBlue: Bummer. So about today . . . We were supposed to hit the vintage stores on Melrose Ave.

Darcy1: Yes. Shopping therapy.

TruBlue: Think about it. Do Lindsay and Kathi really want to do that?

Darcy1: No. They'd be bored.

TruBlue: That's what I figured.

Darcyı: But it's Sunday! It's my last day here. If we cancel, I won't see you again. :(

TruBlue: Let's blow off shopping. You come here.
Darcyı: Where?

TruBlue: To my house. Bring the Bailey girls. We can hang, go in the pool. Chill.

Darcyı: Laid-back day?

TruBlue: Exactly.

Darcyı: That sounds perfect!

"How does a day by the pool sound?" Darcy asked Kathi and Lindsay as they chowed down on omelets at the hotel restaurant. "Tru's invited us to her place. She's got a huge pool and a hot tub."

"At her house?" Lindsay asked.

Darcy nodded. "We can just hang out and listen to music and go swimming and sunbathe and relax."

Silence. Darcy sighed. When was she going to accept the fact that her idea of what to do with a day in Los Angeles just didn't match Lindsay and Kathi's idea of what to do?

"I kinda wanted to go to Universal Studios today,"

Kathi admitted. "There's a whole amusement park
there. And they give a tour of the real studio, where they
make movies and everything."

"I know," Darcy said.

"An amusement park sounds like fun," Lindsay put
in.

"Okay." Darcy pulled out her Blackberry. "Let me
just tell Tru I won't be able to see her today after all."

"Why?" Kathi asked. "Won't she come with us?"

"I doubt it," Darcy replied. "Her father works at
Universal. She's been there a gazillion times. And she
changed her plans for us yesterday. I doubt she'll do it
again." She typed in Tru's e-mail address, trying to keep
her voice from shaking. She felt like crying. When her
mom had first told her about visiting L.A., Darcy had
pictured an entire weekend spent with her old friends.
But it seemed like she would end up spending most of
the weekend without them. And who knew when she'd
see Tru again? Or Riley?

"Wait," Kathi said, reaching for the Blackberry.
"Never mind."

"What do you mean?" Darcy asked.

"Never mind Universal Studios," Kathi told her. "I
don't need to go there."

"But you want to see it," Darcy replied. "And so
does Lindsay."

"Yeah, but you want to see Tru," Kathi said. "That's more important. You were nice enough to bring us along on your visit home, and we've been hogging all your time and making you do things you don't want to do."

"That's not true," Darcy protested.

"Yes, it is," Lindsay put in. "You wanted to go to the spa yesterday and instead you spent the day hiking and sightseeing just because we wanted to. And then I got mad at you and acted like a jerk."

"No, you didn't," Darcy said.

"I kinda did," Lindsay replied. "And I'm sorry. You came here to see your old home and your old friends. We haven't been very understanding."

"So forget about Universal Studios," Kathi said. "Let's go hang out at Tru's house instead. You can show us what it's really like to live in Los Angeles. I know you didn't spend much time walking up and down the Walk of Fame or eating at the House of Blues."

"Well . . . no," Darcy admitted. "But I did spend a lot of time vegging by the pool at Tru's!" She jumped up and hugged them both. "Thanks, you guys. I really appreciate this."

By the time Andre dropped them off in Tru's driveway, even Lindsay was smiling. "It's really beautiful here," she said, looking around the tree-covered hillside that rose up next to the house. "Where are we?"

"Bel Air," Darcy said. "This is my favorite neighborhood. Besides Malibu, of course."

Tru threw open the front door of the big Spanish-style house. "Hey, guys!" she called. "Come on in."

"Wow," Kathi said, staring around the huge foyer. "This place is a mansion."

Tru laughed. "Not really. You should've seen Darcy's old house."

"Yeah, but Tru has the pool to die for," Darcy said. "Let me at it!" She led the way through the living room and the gleaming chef's kitchen and out the French doors to the backyard. The pool was irregularly shaped and landscaped to look like a natural lagoon, with flowers and bushes right up to the edge of the water in some places. The tiled walls were a deep dark blue, which made the water look even bluer. On one end there was a raised hot tub, and the water from it spilled over into the regular pool like a little waterfall. The pool house was a small hut with a bamboo roof. A pile of fluffy towels lay on a marble table near the door.

"This isn't what I was expecting," Lindsay said, stopping to take it all in. "I figured it would be like hanging out at the hotel pool, only smaller."

"Nope." Darcy smiled. "Tru's mother is a designer, so she's got the most gorgeous house inside and out."

"Is she here?" Kathi asked.

Tru shook her head. "She's at work. And it's the housekeeper's day off, so it's just us. But I've got plenty of leftover dessert from this party my mother threw last night, so we can pig out if we want! There are even mini éclairs, Darce. Your favorite."

Darcy's stomach did a little happy dance at the thought. "In Bailey they make éclairs with this weird, goopy filling," she said. "I have not had a good éclair since I moved there."

"Or a good latte," Tru reminded her.

"Or sushi," Darcy added. "Or . . ." Suddenly she realized how she must sound to Lindsay and Kathi. They probably thought she was complaining about Bailey or putting it down because it didn't have much in the way of semi-exotic food. Her cheeks heated up, and she shot a guilty look at her friends.

"It's okay, Darcy, we know Bailey isn't the culinary capital of the world," Lindsay told her.

"No, but it's got great . . . bales of hay," Darcy said lamely. "I'm sorry, you guys. You know I love Bailey. I just miss home sometimes, that's all."

"Well, today will be just like old times," Tru said. "So you can fill up on L.A. feelings to live off of for a while back in Bailey."

"Yeah, I'll store it all up like a camel." Darcy grinned. "Did I ever tell you about the camel I met?"

Tru plopped down on one of the pillow-covered stone lounges and kicked off her kitten-heel flip-flops. "There are camels in Bailey?"

"Only one," Kathi said. "These two brothers have a wildlife rehabilitation facility."

"And a camel named Petunia," Darcy said. "She spits."

"All camels spit," Lindsay put in.

"Maybe. But Petunia *aims* and spits," Darcy said.

"Then you should learn to duck." Tru giggled. "Just like in second grade when Jason Williams and Dale Tyson were having that spitting contest and you got in the way."

Kathi's mouth fell open. "What happened?"

"Darcy had been practicing writing her autograph instead of doing her math, so the teacher wanted her to go to the principal at recess. On the way she was walking by these two gross boys. She saw them start to spit, so she ducked down," Tru said. "The spit totally went over her head."

"Unfortunately the teacher was walking with me," Darcy added. "So the spit went over me and hit him!"

Kathi burst out laughing. "Did you get in even bigger trouble?"

"No way," Darcy said. "He was so mad at Jason and Dale that he forgot about me and took them to the principal instead."

They all laughed.

Kathi pulled one of her cameras from her bag. "Do you mind if I take a few pictures of your backyard, Tru?" she asked. "It's so beautiful. I want the people back home to see it."

"Go crazy," Tru said. "There's a rose garden around the side, too, if you want pictures of that. The flowers—" She was interrupted by a loud meow from underneath her lounge chair. "Oops. I was ignoring Mrs. Fluff," Tru said with a laugh. She bent down and picked up a Persian cat who was rubbing against her ankles. The cat settled down on the end of the chair and began to purr.

Darcy gasped. "Mrs. Fluff!" she cried. "I missed her." She leaned over to pet the cat under the chin the way she liked it. "She looks skinnier."

"Yeah, she lost a pound," Tru said. "It makes a big difference when you only weigh twelve pounds to begin with!"

"Hi, Mrs. Fluff," Lindsay said. She went over to kneel next to the cat. "You're beautiful." Mrs. Fluff pushed her head against Lindsay's hand, asking to be petted. Lindsay laughed and glanced up at Darcy. "This place has everything," she said. "A pool for you, scenery for Kathi to take pictures of, and an animal for me to pet. Your house is perfect, Tru!"

"Thanks," Tru said. "I'm glad you guys could come over."

"Me too," Darcy said. "I've been stressed all weekend. But right now I feel totally relaxed!"

"This is even worse than yesterday," Jack complained on Sunday morning. He had come into the kitchen for a glass of water. "There's no way we're going to get all the animals to eat their morning food before it's time to give them their evening meal!"

"I know what you mean," Eli said. "I've been trying to get Dick and Jane to eat for almost an hour. Talk about finicky cats!" He reached into the cat cage set up in one of the corners and shook the food bowl so that the kibble inside rattled. The two tabbies in the cage ignored him.

"Have they eaten anything at all?" Victoria asked, rummaging in the fridge for an apple.

"*Awwwk!* Fatso!" squawked the parrot from his perch atop the counter. He flapped furiously, his wingspan taking up nearly his entire cage.

"Stop that," Victoria told him, taking out an apple. She cut a slice. "It's rude to call people fat."

"I think Jane had one bite of her kibble," Eli said. "But otherwise they've ignored it completely. Dick hasn't eaten a thing."

"That's not good. We've got to get them to eat."
Victoria fed the apple slice to Beaker, who kept flapping
his wings and squawking. "It's almost time for us to
start exercising the dogs."

"Um, I don't know about that," Eli said. "I might
have a little problem with the assembly line today."

"*Awwwk!* Dumb-dumb!" Beaker squawked. He
threw the piece of apple through the bars of his cage.

"I am not dumb!" Victoria cried. "And you have to
eat." She glanced over at Eli. "What's the problem?"

"I can't really move my legs," Eli replied. He
walked stiffly from the cat cage over to the table and
lowered himself down with a groan.

"Eli, whatever is the matter?" Victoria cried,
concerned.

"I think I did a little too much jogging yesterday,"
Eli said. "The dogs were only running for ten minutes
each, but I was going for two hours straight!"

Victoria frowned. "I didn't think of that."

"Every muscle in my body hurts," Eli moaned.

"Wimpy!" squawked the parrot.

"That's enough," Victoria said. "I'm going to teach
you something to say other than insults."

"Like what?" Jack asked.

Victoria thought about it for a moment. "I know!
I'll teach him a song."

"*Awwwk!* Loser!" Beaker crowed.

"If I were a rich man," Victoria sang.

The parrot looked at her and cocked his head.

"If I were a rich man," she sang again.

"*Awwwk!* If I were a rich man!" Beaker sang.

"If I were a rich man," Victoria sang. "Ya ha deedle deedle, bubba bubba deedle deedle *dum*."

"Dumb-dumb!"

Jack and Eli laughed. "Hmm. I should have thought of that," Victoria murmured. "If I were a rich man," she tried again. "Ya ha deedle deedle, bubba bubba deedle deedle dum."

"If I were a rich man," Beaker sang. "Dumb-dumb!"

"That's good enough for me," Victoria said. She gave him another slice of the apple, and he gobbled it down.

"One problem solved," Jack said. "But what about Dick and Jane? And exercising the dogs?"

"*Awwwk!* If I were a rich man. Dumb-dumb!" Beaker sang loudly.

Victoria pulled a can of tuna fish down from a cabinet and stuck it in the can opener. "Can you jog with any of the dogs, Eli?" she asked.

"I might be able to hobble a little with some of the smaller dogs," Eli replied.

"Hmm. That won't help terribly much, I'm afraid. Although I appreciate the offer." Victoria opened the cat cage and poured the water from the tuna over Dick and Jane's food. Immediately both cats came running for the food bowl.

"Wow. Good thinking," Jack said, watching the tabbies gobble down their kibble.

"Make it taste like tuna, and a cat will eat it every time," Victoria said. "Well, *almost* every time."

"If I were a rich man!" Beaker squawked.

"The dogs need their exercise. I think we're going to have to call for reinforcements." Victoria reached for the phone.

"Who?" Jack asked.

"The Brennan brothers," Victoria said. "They always have their hands full with all their own animals, but I'm sure they'd be willing to come over and walk dogs for a few hours. It is an emergency, after all."

"If you and Brett and Brandon can take all the big dogs for a long hike, I can manage to take the little ones for shorter walks," Eli said. "I'll just stand still and let them walk in circles around me."

Jack shook his head. It was way too easy to picture Eli getting tied up in leashes that way. Apparently Victoria was thinking the same thing, because she didn't look too convinced. "You'll be careful, won't you? I don't want you getting even more hurt."

"They're tiny dogs. How bad could it be?" Eli said.

"All right." Victoria dialed and got Brett Brennan on the phone. As soon as she'd explained the situation, he agreed to come right over with his brother. "That's all settled," she said when she hung up. "I'll begin rounding up the big dogs so we can start hiking as soon as they arrive. Eli, you begin exercising the little ones . . . *carefully*."

"Great," Eli said. He got slowly to his feet and hobbled off, inching forward and groaning with every step.

"What should I do?" Jack asked.

"Why, you have the same job as yesterday," Victoria told him cheerfully. "Cleaning out all the cages!"

"I can't believe Riley didn't even mention that," Darcy said to Tru. "She was really dating Ty McDonnell?"

"For a whole month," Tru replied. "She was so depressed when they broke up. He dumped her right before the big Carrillo Foundation gala."

"What a jerk," Darcy replied. "Poor Riley. Why didn't she say anything about it?"

"Well, we haven't really had a lot of time to talk this weekend," Tru pointed out. "It's probably not the kind of thing she wanted to bring up in the middle of Grauman's Chinese Theatre."

Darcy bit her lip. She hated to think about Riley keeping quiet on something upsetting just because they'd been busy entertaining Darcy's new friends from Bailey. The issues between her two sets of friends just kept coming up. And now she probably wouldn't even see Riley again before she left.

Kathi was asleep on her lounge chair, and Lindsay was swimming laps in the pool. Darcy had been so happy when she first found out they could come to California with her. But maybe it would've been better for everybody if she'd come out to Los Angeles by herself.

"What about you, Darce?" Tru asked, leaning over the side of her chair to pick up Mrs. Fluff. "How are you, really? Do you like it in Bailey? It sounds boring."

"It's been boring lately," Darcy said. "But between the animals on our ranch and the animals at the vet's office, things are usually hopping. You wouldn't believe how busy a bunch of beasts can keep you!"

"Oh, yes, I would," Tru replied. "The Fluffmeister here has been keeping me seriously busy lately. You know how I use that kitty litter that clumps up when she pees?"

Darcy nodded. "Then you just scoop out the little balls of litter, right?"

"I used to. But lately her whole litter box is like one humongous clump! She must be peeing *a lot*." Tru made a face. "I don't know what's going on with her— maybe she's got a drinking problem!"

Darcy laughed.

"You should see me," Tru went on, grinning. "I practically have to get a shovel to scoop it all out."

"Then I bet you'd be awesome at mucking out stables," Darcy told her. "We use pitchforks instead of shovels, but it's the same basic idea."

"And you do that every day?"

"You know it," Darcy said. "It's amazing how not gross it starts to seem after a while."

Tru looked skeptical. "I still think Mrs. Fluff's litter box is pretty gross." She kissed the cat on the head. "You're lucky I love you," she said in baby talk. "Otherwise you'd never have a clean box!"

Darcy leaned back on her lounge and looked at the crystal-clear blue sky. It was always like that in Los Angeles—sunny and clear. "I forgot how perfect the weather is here," she commented.

"Best in the world," Tru agreed. She hesitated. "So . . . do you think your mom is ever going to come back to Hollywood?"

"I doubt it," Darcy said. "She's completely happy in Bailey. You should see her—every day she's into some new thing like gardening or rescuing wildlife or going camping. She's like a little kid, excited about every-thing."

"And what about you?" Tru pressed.

"I'm not so sure," Darcy admitted. "I wanted to hate it there, but I don't. Bailey is pretty cool. It's not as exciting as living here, but I love working at the vet's office, and I love our ranch. And I've made some really great friends."

Mrs. Fluff gave an indignant meow, and Tru quickly began scratching her behind the ears. She kept her eyes on the cat, but Darcy could tell her mind was on some-thing else. "Are they better friends than you have here?" she asked, not looking up.

"Are you kidding?" Darcy cried. "Of course not. Nobody could ever be more important to me than you guys. And being back here has reminded me how much I miss you guys and how much I miss my old life. But I like my new life, too."

"So you're really gonna stay there, huh?" Tru asked wistfully. "I kept hoping it was only temporary."

"I think it's permanent," Darcy said. "And I think I'm okay with that. Life on the ranch suits me." She took in her friend's gloomy expression, and her own heart gave a sad little thump. "But you know, Bailey is never going to be *exactly* what I want, because it doesn't have you."

"Then maybe you *should* move back here," Lindsay snapped.

Darcy jumped and turned around. Lindsay stood there frowning, a hurt expression in her hazel eyes. Darcy quickly ran back over everything she'd just said. She hadn't said anything bad about Lindsay, had she?

Or maybe Lindsay had only heard the very last thing she'd said.

"Linds, I wasn't saying—"

"Oh, no!" Tru's voice was shrill. "Darcy, help!"

Darcy spun toward her friend. "What? What's wrong?"

"It's Mrs. Fluff," Tru cried. "Look at her. She just collapsed. She's unconscious!"

Chapter 8

> Wild Wisdom . . . *Domestic cats purr during both inhalation and exhalation. Big cats, like lions and tigers, have a "one-way purr" when they breathe out.*

"What's wrong with her?" Tru wailed, bending anxiously over the Persian cat. "Mrs. Fluff! Wake up!"

But the cat just laid there. Her eyes were open and glassy, and her breathing was shallow.

Kathi rushed over, rubbing sleep from her eyes. When she saw Mrs. Fluff, she gasped in horror. The cat looked really bad.

"Omigosh, Darcy, what's happening?" Tru began to cry. "What should I do?"

"Did she eat anything weird?" Darcy asked frantically. "What was she doing right before she collapsed?"

"Nothing," Tru said. "She was sitting there, and I was petting her, and suddenly she sort of . . . I don't know, got stiff. And then she fell over."

"What do you mean, stiff?" Lindsay asked calmly.

"Her legs kind of kicked out," Tru said. "I don't know how to describe it."

Lindsay shot a look at Darcy. "Didn't you say Mrs. Fluff had been losing weight lately?"

Darcy nodded, starting to get an idea of what Lindsay was thinking. "Yes! Tru, you said she'd lost a pound. Was she on a diet?" Darcy asked.

"No," Tru replied.

"And her litter box has been weird—superclumpy—lately," Darcy told Lindsay. "Tru says she's been urinating a lot."

Lindsay nodded. "Diabetic reaction," she said. "We need sugar."

Tru was still bent over the cat, petting her and begging her to wake up. Darcy could tell her friend wasn't going to be much use right now—she was too upset. "I'll get it," she told Lindsay. She jumped up and ran into the kitchen, making a beeline for the cabinet with all the breakfast cereal. It was a good thing she'd spent so many nights sleeping over here. She knew just where to look.

Darcy yanked open the cherrywood cabinet and pushed aside three boxes of muesli and some Cap'n Crunch. There, behind the cereal, was a bottle of maple syrup for pancakes. Darcy grabbed it and ran back out to the pool. "Syrup," she panted.

"Good. Tru, back up a little and let me get to Mrs. Fluff's mouth," Lindsay said in a relaxed, no-nonsense voice. Tru listened to her without hesitation, putting the cat down on the lounge chair and backing away.

Lindsay gently pulled Mrs. Fluff's lips away from her teeth, revealing a stretch of gum. Darcy poured the syrup onto her finger and rubbed it onto the cat's gums. "More?" she asked.

Lindsay nodded. Darcy applied some more syrup, putting it on the top and bottom gums, and on the inside of the cat's mouth when Lindsay opened it wider.

"Don't worry. They know what they're doing," Kathi told Tru, slipping an arm around her shoulders. "It will work."

But for a long moment, nothing changed. Mrs. Fluff still lay there, stiff and unconscious, her eyes open and staring at nothing.

Please wake up, Fluffy, Darcy silently begged her. *Don't let us be too late.*

Suddenly Mrs. Fluff blinked. Then blinked again. And then let out a long, deep meow. She lifted her head and looked around woozily.

"Oh, thank God!" Tru cried. She dropped to her knees next to the chair and kissed the cat on the head. "You're back!"

"What happened to her?" Kathi asked. "Did you guys say she was diabetic?"

Lindsay nodded. "Most likely, she was having a low-blood-sugar reaction. So when we got some sugar into her system, she came around."

"How did you know?" Tru asked, stroking Mrs. Fluff's soft fur.

"All that clumping in the litter box was because Mrs. Fluff has too much sugar in her urine," Lindsay explained. "And lots of cats will lose weight when they become diabetic. So she had two symptoms, and then the way she collapsed matched the description of a diabetic reaction."

"But she's not diabetic," Tru said. "I mean, she never has been."

"Cats are weird," Darcy told her. "They can turn diabetic at any time."

"It's true," Lindsay said. "Sometimes they're diabetic for a while, and then they go back to being nondiabetic. It makes them pretty hard to treat."

"Well, you didn't seem to have a problem treating Mrs. Fluff," Tru replied. "Did you guys just save her life?"

Darcy glanced at Lindsay. "I don't know if I would've come up with diabetes on my own," she

131

admitted. "But Lindsay definitely just saved her life."

Tru stared at Lindsay, wide-eyed. "I can't believe it," she said. "Thank you so much."

Lindsay blushed a little. "Darcy's exaggerating."

"I don't think so," Tru said. "You're like a professional or something. I was freaking out, but you stayed totally calm."

"She gets it from her father," Kathi put in. "You should see him whenever there's a sick animal to treat— he's always completely relaxed and in control."

"You should be a vet, too," Tru told Lindsay. "You'd be great at it."

"We'll see," Lindsay said. "I still have a lot to learn. But I do know one thing: Mrs. Fluff isn't out of the woods yet."

Tru's eyebrows shot up. "What do you mean?"

"Look at her. She's still really out of it," Darcy said. The Persian was lying on her side, her breathing shallow. Whenever she tried to pick up her head, it flopped around like a rag doll's.

"We've managed to prevent her from going into a coma," Lindsay said.

"A coma?" Tru cried.

"That's what happens if you don't stop the reaction," Lindsay explained. "But now you need to deal with what's *causing* the reaction. You have to get Mrs. Fluff's diabetes under control—and fast. We did what we could at home, but she needs to see a vet right away."

Darcy pulled out her cell and hit a preprogrammed number. "I'm paging Andre to tell him to come get us ASAP. He can take us straight to the vet."

"No, he can't," Tru said. "My vet isn't open on Sundays."

"So what are we going to do?" Kathi cried.

"There must be an emergency veterinary center," Lindsay said. "Do you know where it is?"

Tru shook her head. "I've never had a veterinary emergency before."

"Can we look one up online?" Kathi asked.

"I have a better idea." Darcy began dialing her cell again. "I know someone who will definitely have all the info on every emergency vet in town."

"Who?" Lindsay asked.

"Riley," Tru said. She smiled at Darcy. "Good thinking. Riley takes Duchess to emergency centers all the time. No matter where she is, if Duchess has an asthma attack, Riley runs straight to the vet."

"Duchess is asthmatic?" Lindsay said. "I didn't know that."

Darcy nodded, listening as Riley's phone rang. "Hello?" her friend said. "Darce?"

"Yeah, it's me," Darcy replied. "We need your help.

Mrs. Fluff had a diabetic reaction, and we need to get her to a vet."

Riley gasped. "Is she okay?"

Darcy glanced at the cat. She looked much better than she had earlier, but she was still clearly a very sick kitty. "She will be if we can find an emergency vet," Darcy told Riley, hoping it was true.

"Are you at Tru's?" Riley asked.

"Yup."

"Okay. The closest one is near UCLA, on Sepulveda Boulevard. They're open twenty-four-seven."

"You're a lifesaver, Ri," Darcy told her. "Thank you." She hung up with Riley and turned back to Tru. "Do you have a carrying case for Mrs. Fluff?"

"I'd rather just carry her in my arms." Tru hesitated. "Is it safe to pick her up?"

"Sure," Lindsay said. "Just be gentle and support her head—she's very weak right now. But being close to you will make her feel better. She won't be as scared."

As they went into the house, Darcy heard the sound of a car pulling up outside. "Andre's here," she told Tru. "He'll get us to the vet before Mrs. Fluff gets any worse."

She only hoped she was right.

Chapter 9

"This is really serious, isn't it?" Tru asked quietly as they whizzed through the streets on the way to the vet. "I can tell by your face, Darcy. You have those little frown lines pointing down from your mouth."

Darcy put her hand over her mouth. "I do not!"

"Yes, you do, you always get them when you're worried." Tru nuzzled Mrs. Fluff's head, but the cat didn't respond. "Tell me the truth. Fluff might still die, right?"

Darcy sighed. She didn't want Tru to panic, but she had to be honest with her friend. "It's possible," she admitted. "One of the big things I've learned working with Lindsay and her dad is that cats are unpredictable. They can be supersick, and you won't even know it because they act normal. They don't show symptoms."

Tru's eyes filled with tears.

"But sometimes cats are totally out of it and look as if they won't make it through the night," Darcy hurried on. "And then when you check on them the next day, they're a hundred times better. They really do have nine lives." She reached over and scratched under Mrs. Fluff's chin. "Don't you, girl?"

"I thought when she woke up that the whole thing was over," Tru said, her voice trembling. "I guess not."

"Try to stay positive," Darcy told her. "Plenty of cats have diabetes, if that's what it is. Things could be a lot worse. Mrs. Fluff is hanging in there, and we're almost at the vet's."

"Thanks." Tru smiled wanly. "I don't know what I would've done without you today. You're really good at this stuff now, huh?"

"Not as good as Lindsay," Darcy said. "But I've been around enough sick animals to pick up a thing or two. Who ever would've thought I'd have such an important job?"

"Well, I'm glad you do," Tru said. "You really helped me today."

"We're here," Kathi said from the other side of the limo. "We're pulling into the parking lot."

They barely waited for the car to stop before they all leaped out. Kathi ran to hold the front door open, while Lindsay hurried up to the counter to talk to the receptionist. Darcy stayed with Tru as they walked slowly inside, trying to move Mrs. Fluff as little as possible.

"Okay, I explained the situation. They're going to take her right into the back," Lindsay told them, coming over from the desk.

"Can I go back there with her?" Tru asked.

Lindsay shook her head. "No. But don't worry. That's normal."

"The vets need to check her out and do some tests," Darcy explained. "You'd only be in their way. They know what they're doing. They'll take good care of her."

Tru nodded uncertainly. "I still wish I could be with her."

A woman in scrubs printed with little dogs and cats rushed out the swinging door next to the front desk. "Mrs. Fluff?" she asked.

"Right here," Tru said.

"I'm Dr. Aberman," the vet introduced herself. "I'll take your kitty back now. I hear she had a low-blood-sugar reaction?"

"Yes," Darcy said. "We put maple syrup on her gums, and she woke up, but she's still majorly out of it."

Dr. Aberman nodded. "She's a lot better than she

would've been if you hadn't given her some sugar. We'll see if we can get her glucose levels regulated now."

Tru gingerly handed the Persian over to the vet, and they all watched as Dr. Aberman disappeared behind the door.

"What do I do now?" Tru asked.

"Now we wait," Lindsay told her. "Let's sit down."

Darcy took Tru's arm and guided her over to the couches set up in the waiting room. She had no idea how long they were going to be here, but she knew there was no way she would leave Tru's side until they heard from the vet.

Suddenly the front door burst open and Riley came running inside. Her long, dark hair was a mess, and her button-down shirt was buttoned wrong. She scanned the waiting room, then made a beeline for Tru. "How's Mrs. Fluff?" she asked, hugging Tru. "What happened?"

"I hardly even understand it," Tru admitted. "These guys are the ones who know what's going on."

Riley gave Darcy a questioning look. "Mrs. Fluff collapsed," Darcy said. "Actually, I guess technically she had a kind of seizure. Right, Linds?"

Lindsay nodded. "That's why her legs were so stiff."

"She was completely unconscious," Tru said. "It was terrifying."

Riley's eyes widened. "It sounds awful. I can't imagine what I would do if that happened to Duchess."

"Lindsay figured out that Mrs. Fluff needed sugar," Tru went on. "She and Darcy totally saved her."

"What did the vet say?" Riley asked.

"Nothing yet," Darcy replied. "They're examining her now."

"Which doctor is it?"

"Dr. Aberman," Lindsay said.

"Great!" Riley cried. "She's my favorite vet here. This one time, Duchess had such a bad attack that her tongue was purple. I was freaking out, but Dr. Aberman just took her in and gave her a shot and everything was fine. She's the one who explained all about asthma to me."

"How long has Duchess been asthmatic?" Lindsay asked.

"Two years," Riley said.

"It's rare in dogs," Lindsay told her.

"I know. Poor little Duchess just got unlucky," Riley replied.

"Looks to me like she's very lucky," Lindsay said. "She has you. A lot of people wouldn't know how to handle a pet with a chronic condition like that. But you obviously take good care of her."

"I try." Riley plopped down on the couch.

"I owe you an apology," Lindsay told her. "I was

wrong to criticize you yesterday about carrying Duchess in your purse."

"Everybody does that here."

"I know, that's what you and Darcy said. I should've listened to you," Lindsay said. "I just thought I knew better because my father's a vet. But I can see that you're an animal lover, too. You wouldn't do something that's bad for your dog."

"Well, she gets tired when she runs around. And sometimes that leads to an asthma attack," Riley said. "So if I'm going to be out all day, Duchess rides in my bag. That way she's not as tired."

"It must be tough, always being afraid that she'll have an asthma attack," Lindsay said sympathetically.

"It is," Riley confirmed. "But I've sure learned a lot about asthma. And dogs."

"That's how I learn, too," Lindsay told her. "Just by seeing the sick animals and watching how my father treats them."

The swinging door opened again and Dr. Aberman came back out.

"How's Mrs. Fluff?" Tru asked, jumping to her feet.

"She's resting," the vet said. "We checked the level of glucose in her blood, and your friends were right. It looks as if she's become diabetic. It's a good thing you girls knew to give her syrup."

"Will she live?" Tru asked anxiously.

"Yes," Dr. Aberman said. "We've got her on an IV now to get more sugar into her. It's astonishing how fast it works. Your kitty is alert and meowing already."

Darcy and her friends all cheered.

"Can I see her?" Tru asked.

"Absolutely. Come on back." Dr. Aberman held the door open for Tru. "I'm sorry there's not enough room back there for all you girls."

"We'll wait out here for you, Tru," Riley said.

"Take as long as you want," Darcy added. She was so relieved to hear that Mrs. Fluff was okay that she wouldn't mind hanging out in the vet's office all day.

"Wow. You totally called the diabetes thing," Riley said to Lindsay. "You saved Mrs. Fluff's life!"

"Well, you helped," Lindsay replied. "You knew where the closest vet was so we could get here as fast as possible. Without that IV we might still have lost Mrs. Fluff."

They smiled at each other as they plopped down on the waiting-room couch.

Darcy could hardly believe her eyes. Finally her friends were getting along!

Chapter 10

Kevin jumped out of his pickup on Sunday evening and stretched his arms over his head. With a happy sigh, he headed over to the door of Victoria's ranch house, knocked twice, and let himself in.

"Great news!" he called. "Bingo has made it through the worst of the distemper!"

"That's wonderful," Victoria's voice called. Kevin stopped and looked around the living room. Animals slumbered in cages everywhere, but there was no sign of Victoria, Jack, or Eli.

"Where is everybody?" he asked.

"Kitchen," Jack replied.

Kevin bounded into the kitchen, where they were all gathered around the table. "So it looks as if Bingo will make it. And the other three dogs, as well," he told them. "I managed to get them all transferred to the animal hospital in Boulder, now that they're well enough to move. Bingo may end up having a little blindness, but, you know, that's often a side effect of the secondary infections caused by distemper. He's still a very lucky dog."

"Good job, Dad," Jack said wanly.

"Thanks. I'm pretty proud of myself," Kevin admitted. "Distemper is very serious. Thankfully it's very rare these days, but there's no real cure. So getting not just one, but *four* dogs through it is hard to do. You should've seen us—Annie and her staff and me. Boy, we were working like . . . well, like dogs." He laughed at his little joke. "Get it?"

"Yeah. Funny." Eli didn't sound amused, but Kevin ignored that.

"I mean, we were constantly busy," Kevin said. "You can't even imagine how exhausted I am."

"Oh, I think we can imagine what it's like to be busy," Victoria said.

"No, I mean we were running around like crazy, giving medicine and handling IV lines, cleaning up after the dogs—"

"We can imagine *that*, too," Jack interrupted.

"Oh. Well, now that the dogs are off to Boulder, we've been disinfecting the whole kennel. Annie's

workers are finishing up right now. So we can move all
the animals back over there first thing in the morning, and
you guys can get to relax a little," Kevin said. "Unless you
want to keep them a little longer?"

"No!" they all shouted at once.

Kevin stepped back, shocked by their outburst.
"What's going on?" he asked. He studied their faces.

Victoria had deep bags under her eyes.

Eli was yawning.

Jack had smudges of dirt all over his cheeks.

And now that he took a good look at them, Kevin
noticed some other weird things as well: Eli had ice packs
tied to his legs and kept grimacing every time he moved,
Victoria's khakis had muddy paw prints all over them,
and Jack smelled like a dog's cage.

And the parrot on the counter kept singing "If I
Were a Rich Man."

"What on earth have you all been doing?" Kevin
asked. "You look terrible. You smell terrible!"

"*Awwwk!* Stuff it!" the parrot squawked.

They all laughed. "We'll have the animals loaded in
the pickup and ready to go the second Annie is done
disinfecting McCormick's McBoardinghouse," Victoria
told him. "I promise."

"That is the cutest sweater I've ever seen," Lindsay

said on Sunday night. She reached out to stroke the faux-fur collar of Riley's cardigan.

Darcy and Kathi stared at her.

"What?" Lindsay asked. "I like fashion. Sometimes."

"Thanks," Riley said. "I got it at this adorable little boutique on Melrose Avenue. Next time you guys come out to L.A., we have to go there."

Darcy smiled and glanced out the window of the limo. The lights of Santa Monica were flying by. "I hope we get to the pier before the sun totally sets," she said. "It's our last night in town, and these Bailey girls have never seen a *real* sunset before!"

"It's true. There's nothing better than watching the sun sink into the ocean," Tru said.

Kathi bounced up and down, excited. "I can't wait to stick my feet into the Pacific. That's the only thing left on my list of stuff to do in California."

"Really? We did your whole list?" Darcy asked. "What about Universal Studios?"

"And Disneyland?" Lindsay added.

"And meeting Ashton Kutcher?" Darcy said.

"Well . . . I kinda shortened the list," Kathi replied. "Obviously one weekend wasn't going to be enough time to do all that. Not if we wanted to hang with the girls, too."

"There's a lot more stuff to put on that list," Riley said. "Tourists don't get to see the real Los Angeles. You know, the things we natives like to do."

"Next time we should go to the Getty Center," Tru said. "It has the best views!"

"And we need to see a movie in the Cinerama Dome," Darcy added.

"And go shopping at Amoeba Records," Riley said.

Kathi frowned. "I hope we didn't bore you guys too much wanting to do all the tourist stuff."

"We did some nontouristy things," Darcy told her. "Like hiking in Runyon Canyon."

"And spending two hours at the vet's," Tru joked.

"Well, if that's what you like to do, you should come visit us in Bailey," Lindsay teased her. "We spend *a lot* of time at the vet's!"

"I would love to visit Bailey," Riley said.

"Me too," Tru agreed.

Darcy couldn't believe her ears. "You would?"

"Sure. If you ever invite us," Tru said.

"I didn't think you'd want to come," Darcy admitted. "I figured you guys would think it was boring."

"With all those animals?" Riley cried. "How could it be boring? Just seeing your mother on a ranch would be worth the trip!"

"Victoria is amazing at running the ranch," Kathi said. "She's a natural."

"Could we go horseback riding there?" Tru asked.

"Absolutely," Darcy said. "We could go elephant-back riding if you want. The Brennan brothers have a rescued circus elephant named Lulu!"

"She loves giving rides," Kathi added. "She used to do it all the time, and now she misses it."

"An elephant? Wow." Riley's eyes were troubled. "Do they have a whole habitat for her? It's very important for an elephant to have lots of room."

"Don't worry. She's got a great home," Lindsay said. "My dad helped them design her habitat. He was on the Internet researching the best wildlife preserves in the world. Lulu's got everything she needs."

"The Brennans noticed her getting depressed, and that's when they realized she misses doing her circus tricks," Darcy explained. "So they let people ride her sometimes. But only if she seems into it."

The limo pulled to a stop at the end of the Santa Monica Pier. "Everybody out," Andre called from the front. "I'll pick you ladies up at nine thirty."

"That's too early," Darcy told him. "How about eleven?"

Andre grinned at her and shook his head. "I have strict orders from your mother. She said you'll have at least an hour of packing to do later, and your flight is very early tomorrow morning. I'm not allowed to let you stay out late tonight."

Darcy rolled her eyes. "Is she afraid I'm gonna over-sleep and miss the plane?"

"You've missed almost every early-morning flight in your life," Andre said. "And don't think I don't know it!"

Darcy made a face, and her friends laughed. "All right, see you at nine thirty," she grumbled. Andre took off with a wave.

"We better hurry if we want to watch the sunset," Tru said. "Let's go out to the end of the pier."

They made their way down the crowded wooden pier, passing little booths that sold kites, statuettes, beach
towels, and jewelry.

"Hang on," Kathi said. "Let me just get a picture of this. This booth sells marionettes!" She whipped out one of her cameras and started to focus.

Darcy gently pulled her away. "We'll miss the sunset if you stop to take photos."

"How about just one?" Kathi said. "Look at that booth—they'll print my name on a grain of rice!" She lifted the camera to her eye, then lowered it. "Why would I want my name on rice?"

"Take a picture on the way back," Darcy suggested. She linked arms with Kathi to keep her moving, and they followed Tru, Riley, and Lindsay toward the end of the pier. By the time they got there, the entire western sky was a bright shade of pink. Streaks of orange shot through the pink haze, and the sun itself was a ball of liquid fire.

"Look at the water," Lindsay gasped. A trail of orange ripples seemed to lead directly from the sun to where they were standing.

"I have to get a picture of this," Kathi said.

"Oh, no, you don't." Darcy took the camera from her. "This is something you experience, not something you watch through a little glass window."

"But—"

"Think of it this way," Tru put in. "Do you want to remember the sunset? Or do you want to remember taking pictures of the sunset?"

Kathi grinned. "I guess you're right. I'd rather see the whole thing with my own eyes."

All five of them stood in silence while the sun dipped slowly into the water, its round ball getting distorted on the bottom, as if the light were melting into the sea. Finally it vanished, leaving behind a purplish pink sky.

Darcy sighed. "I miss that," she said. Then she smiled. "But in Bailey you can see more stars at night than I've ever seen in L.A."

"Even at the Oscars?" Kathi joked.

Darcy stuck her tongue out at her. "You know what I mean."

149

"I'm going to call the vet and check on the Fluffster," Tru said, dialing her cell.

"Let's get ice cream," Riley suggested. "There's a place about halfway down the pier that has the best pistachio ever."

"I *love* pistachio," Kathi declared, following her back along the boardwalk. "Do they have waffle cones?"

"You bet," Riley said. "I saw Justin Timberlake eating one of their pistachio cones last month. That's how I know he has good taste."

Kathi caught her breath. "You saw Justin?"

Riley nodded.

"Who else have you seen?"

"Lots of people," Riley said. "You see celebrities all over here. But my favorite was this one time I took Duchess to the dog park and I sat on a bench next to George Clooney. He was there with his dog."

Kathi looked as if she might faint. "Did you talk to him?"

"Even better," Riley said. "He was on the phone the whole time, so I got to listen to him have a fight with his girlfriend. I got the whole scoop, and I knew they were breaking up even before the gossip magazines!"

Trailing behind them, Lindsay shook her head. "I don't know why anybody reads those things," she said.

"Me neither," Darcy replied. "I just like to look at the pictures."

Lindsay laughed. "I guess that's okay." She glanced over as Tru stuck her cell phone back in her jeans pocket. "How's Mrs. Fluff?"

"She's asleep," Tru reported. "Dr. Aberman says her blood-sugar levels are in the normal range now, and they're going to check them again in two hours. I wonder when I'll be able to bring her home."

"Probably in a day or two," Lindsay told her. "They'll want to watch her for a while. Sometimes with cats, their blood sugar goes up and down unpredictably. And it will take them some time to figure out exactly what the right dosage of insulin is."

Tru's eyebrows drew together. "Insulin?"

"You'll probably have to give Mrs. Fluff insulin shots," Darcy said.

"I don't know how to do that!" Tru cried.

"It's easy," Lindsay said. "You just pull up the ruff of her neck and stick the little needle into the loose skin there. It doesn't hurt her at all."

"Are you sure?" Tru sounded worried. "I couldn't stand it if I had to hurt her."

"It's just a short little needle, and it only needs to go right under the skin," Lindsay said. "I promise Mrs. Fluff will barely even feel it."

"Don't worry, Tru. Even I know how to give insulin shots," Darcy said. "You'll have no problem at all."

Tru sighed. "It's all kind of overwhelming."

"You'll get used to it," Lindsay assured her. "Lots of cats have diabetes, and they live perfectly normal lives. I bet Mrs. Fluff will be even happier and healthier now. She was feeling sick, and you didn't even know it. Now she'll be better."

They'd reached the ice-cream shop. Riley and Kathi were already in line, still talking about celebrity sightings.

"I'm not as good at this stuff as you are," Tru said to Lindsay. "I saw how calm you were this afternoon. I don't know if I'll ever be able to deal with it the way you do."

"If you start to freak out, just call me," Lindsay offered. "I'll talk you through it."

"Really?" Tru asked, relieved. "I would love that."

"Of course," Lindsay said. "And when you come to Bailey, I'll introduce you to the two diabetic cats I know there. They've both been living with the disease for more than five years, and they're totally happy."

They're happy? Not as happy as I am, Darcy thought. In fact, she was too happy to even say a word. She just stood rooted to the wooden boardwalk, soaking up the wonderful feelings. This was exactly what she had dreamed of when she first found out she was coming back to California.

Her new friends and her old friends . . . acting like *friends!*

Chapter 11

Wild Wisdom . . . *Iguanas can hold their breath for as long as thirty minutes.*

"*Awwwk!* If I were a rich man!" Beaker squawked.

"Dumb-dumb," Victoria sang along with him. She carefully placed the parrot's cage into the back of Kevin's pickup truck on Monday morning. "Good-bye, you lovely bird," she added.

"Bye-bye!" the parrot cawed. "If I were a rich man!"

"I'm gonna miss these guys," Eli said, hobbling over with Dick and Jane in their cat cage. "And all the dogs, too."

"Enough to keep them here for another couple of days?" Jack asked. "And jog with them all every day?"

"No!" Eli yelped. "Not *that* much." He hurried back toward the house, wincing with every step.

Victoria smiled. "Eli, you should go home and rest

those sore muscles," she called after him. "This is the last truckload of animals. We'll take it from here."

"Really? Thanks." Eli turned quickly toward her, but his legs buckled, and he toppled over sideways. "Um . . . maybe I'll wait a few minutes first."

Kevin stuck his head out the driver's side window. "See you later, Eli. Thanks for all your help!"

"No problem." Eli gave them a weak wave.

Jack and Victoria climbed into the cab, and Kevin pulled slowly down the driveway and out onto the road. He eased the truck over the bumps and uneven pavement in the street, making sure not to jostle the animals in the back.

"Well, I for one am very impressed with the job we've done these past few days," Victoria said, ruffling Jack's hair. "It wasn't easy, but we managed to take care of dogs, cats, reptiles, and rodents all weekend, all by ourselves."

"How about you, Jack? Feel proud of yourself?" Kevin asked.

"I guess so," Jack said. "It's nice to know we helped animals who needed us." He glanced at Victoria, a gleam in his eye. "In fact, this weekend has given me a great idea for a business."

"Uh-oh. Dare I even ask what the idea is?" Victoria teased.

"A kennel," Jack said. "Just think about it—a posh pet boarding center in your very own ranch house."

"In *my* ranch house?"

"It's perfect!" Jack proclaimed. "That big house, the riding ring out back, the barn . . . I mean, we wouldn't put the cages all over the way we did this weekend. We'd convert part of the garage and have built-in cages. And we'd find a room or two in the house for the small-er cages. Maybe one room for cats and another room for exotic animals like snakes and iguanas."

Victoria shot a look at Kevin. He was shaking his head and smiling. Jack hated when adults acted as if he were crazy. He wasn't crazy—this was his best money-making plan yet!

"Do you really want to compete with Annie?" Victoria asked. "McCormick's McBoardinghouse is a very well-known kennel around here."

"We wouldn't have to compete," Jack said. "We'd be more of a . . . boutique. You know, a dude ranch for pets. Or a spa for pets. Heck, we could even run a boot camp for pets that are out of shape—you could take them hiking like you did yesterday. Eli could run with them."

"I don't think he wants to do *that* again anytime soon," Kevin put in.

"And it doesn't have to be pets from around here,"

Jack rushed on, his vision for the place growing bigger and grander the more he thought about it. "Your Hollywood friends could send their pets here for boarding."

"All the way from California?"

"Absolutely! They're rich, aren't they?" Jack asked. "Whenever they go on vacation, they can ship their pets to you so the pet can have a vacation, too. We'll advertise it as a healthy rural getaway for urban pets— clean air, lots of room to run, the whole deal."

"Well, it sounds absolutely lovely, Jack—" Victoria began.

"Great! You'll be the public face of the place. Eli can do all the exercising and the cage cleaning, and I'll be the manager—"

"But I'm afraid it simply won't work," Victoria continued.

Jack's mouth fell open. "But it's such a great idea! Why won't it work?"

"Well, for one thing, I kind of like my house the way it is," Victoria said. "But the most important reason is that I don't think Eli would survive it if we had a kennel at the ranch!"

"Wake up, girls!" Kevin cried on Monday afternoon. "We're here!"

Darcy rubbed the sleep out of her eyes and realized she was in the crowded cab of Kevin's pickup truck. Kathi dozed with her head on Darcy's shoulder, and Lindsay was just waking up on her other side. "How long was I out?" Darcy asked.

"For the whole ride from the airport," Kevin said. "All three of you conked out the second we hit the road."

Kathi yawned and slowly sat up straight. "We had a really busy weekend," she explained.

"You don't say," Kevin replied dryly.

"Check it out—a banner!" Darcy said excitedly. She pointed to the door of the ranch house, where Victoria, Jack, and Eli were waiting. Over their heads was a homemade banner that read, "Welcome Home, California Girls!"

"That is so sweet," Kathi said as they climbed out of the truck.

"They probably spent all weekend making it," Darcy guessed. "Just to give themselves something to do around here!"

"Good. I'm glad we could help them find something to ease the boredom," Lindsay replied. "I do feel a tiny bit bad that I got to have an exciting weekend trip while Jack was stuck in Bailey twiddling his thumbs."

"Hello, darling!" Victoria cried, rushing over to give Darcy a big hug. "Did you have a wonderful time?"

"We totally did," Darcy replied. "Thank you so much, Mom."

"Yeah, thanks, Ms. Fields," Kathi added. "I'll be able to make a fifty-page photo album just from this one weekend!"

"Who's hungry?" Eli interrupted. "Did you guys eat on the plane?"

"No," Darcy replied. "And I'm starving!"

"Me too," Lindsay said.

"Come inside for cake." Eli held the door open wide.

"Cake?" Darcy rushed in, her friends right on her heels. She couldn't believe her eyes—the entire dining room was filled with balloons and the table was all set. A big lopsided cake sat in the middle. It was decorated with icing that read "Welcome Back." The last two letters of "Welcome" drifted down the side of the cake because there was no room on top.

"It's beautiful, Eli," Darcy told him. "Did you make it?"

"Yup. It's all chocolate inside."

"My favorite!" Lindsay cried.

They all sat down, and Eli served up big slices of the cake. Darcy couldn't help but smile. She hadn't expected their homecoming to be such a big deal. Things must have been *really* slow in Bailey for her mother and her friends to spend so much time on a welcome-home celebration.

"Tell us everything," Victoria said. "How was California?"

"It was amazing. I'm pretty sure I saw Julia Roberts. Oh, and I got Dylan Strong's autograph!" Kathi said. "And we went to the Walk of Fame and Grauman's Chinese Theatre and Malibu and Bel Air—"

"And we went hiking, and we went to the Santa Monica Pier, and we helped save Tru's cat," Lindsay butted in.

"Wow. It sounds as if you packed a lot into only a few days," Victoria said.

"You wouldn't believe it," Darcy told her.

"We were a little busy ourselves," Eli replied.

"What did you do all weekend?" Lindsay asked, her brow wrinkled in confusion.

"Let's see. We quarantined an entire kennel, moved about twenty animals from there over to the ranch here, moved the cages over from Creature Comforts . . ." Kevin began.

"Housed, fed, and exercised all the dogs, cats, snakes, chinchillas, iguanas, and the parrot," Victoria continued.

"Exercised all the dogs every day," Eli said.

"And cleaned everybody's cage every day," Jack added.

"All while I treated four more dogs for distemper, saved their lives, and helped to disinfect the entire kennel," Kevin finished.

"Oh, and then we moved them all back to the kennel this morning," Victoria said.

"And then we baked your cake and made the banner," Eli said.

Darcy didn't know what to say. It sounded as if the whole weekend was a disaster in Bailey! How could they all be so cheerful? "Um, good?" she said. "It's nice that you guys had something to keep you busy."

Eli nodded and grinned.

"Anyway, I'm so glad you girls had a good time in Los Angeles," Victoria said. She reached over to smooth Darcy's hair away from her face. "Was it good to be home, sweetie?"

Darcy looked from her mom . . . to her friends' smiling faces . . . to the cake they'd made. Boring as it could be here sometimes, you never knew what was about to happen or when some wacky adventure would start.

"It was nice to see Hollywood again," she said. "But right now it's good to be home. In Bailey."